THE

A NOVEL BY T.L. JAMES

SECRETS REVEALED

Published by PHE Ink
9597 Jones Rd #213
Houston, TX 77065
www.PHEinkPub.com

PHE Ink and the portrayal of the quill feather are trademarks of
PHE Ink.

James, TL, 1971
The MPire: Secrets Revealed: a novel by TL James. – 1st ed.
PHE Ink -2014

Summary: *The MPire: Secrets Revealed* an enchanted journey into
Mallory Haulm's world, as he faces the ultimate reign of power of
biblical proportions filled with family drama and corporate
greed.

ISBN: 978-1-935724-12-4– Print
ISBN: 978-1-935724-63-6 - Ebook
{1. Death – Fiction. 2. Four Horsemen – Fiction 3. Family Saga –
Fiction 4.Austin, TX -- Fiction}

LCCN: On File

Genre: Speculative Fiction/Science Fiction/Family Drama

Printed in the United States of America

I dedicate this book to my father,
Oscar W. James.

4/1927 – 11-2008

SECRETS REVEALED

CHAPTER ONE

Six months had passed since Mallory's debut in running the family business. He thought he made a great impression, although his brothers were confused about his financial questionings. Uncle Mal was pleased to see his efforts and started pressuring him to proselytize, but that was not the case for Marc.

Since Mallory's performance at the company was surprisingly successful, Marc started putting him off. Several times, he went to Marc to ask him about the proselytization process, but Marc refused to answer his questions, insisting that his time was too valuable. So, Mallory decided not to worry about it.

It had also been five months since Mallory made a commitment to Matthew. They finally settled in as a couple, but Mallory was still struggling with his new identity. The guilt of the relationship subsided as Matthew and Mallory became more comfortable with one another. Although keeping the relationship from the family proved to be a painful task, Mallory thought he finally found peace and happiness.

Matthew received an early morning phone call from one of his professors at the University of Oxford. He began a project in college and they needed him to return to complete the research. Matthew was happy but confused by the invitation. After all, he changed his major from Anthropology to Business to spend more with Mallory. To add further confusion, the professor named prominent researchers and senior professors who would be on the team. Matthew was just a director for an energy company mainly because of nepotism. *How could he be of any importance to this team*? The professor was very convincing, even added that the research centered on Matthew's participation, making it hard for him to refuse.

After he got off the phone, he wanted to run to Mallory and tell him the exciting news but he wondered how Mallory would take it. He slipped back into bed without waking him. He laid in the bed anxiously waiting for Mallory to wake up, so they could talk about it. When he finally made his decision, he couldn't wait any longer.

Mallory's brothers developed a habit of dropping by unannounced. Therefore, it was no surprise when Marek came over to tell Mallory personally that Uncle Murphy, whom they all called M-Lee, had been hospitalized. He banged on the door until Peter answered it, then broke through Peter and stormed toward the bedroom. He knew Mallory was still asleep and didn't care if someone was in his bed. He knew Mallory was an exhibitionist and nothing embarrassed him. He opened the door to find Mallory sleeping.

He sat of the edge of the bed and started shaking Mallory until he woke up. Mallory wasn't happy about the visit. All of a sudden, Mallory grabbed the side of the mattress and started shrieking and squirming. Marek couldn't move as he witnessed Mallory cursing loudly, grabbing and squeezing the mattress. He eventually screamed out when Matthew flew from under the covers and kissed him immensely.

Marek was overwhelmed with what he had just witnessed. Mallory couldn't stop Matthew's conquest to tell him about their guest. Matthew moved his conquering move to his neck and shoulders. Mallory grabbed the mattress and cried out again.

Marek was horrified as his eyes froze on Mallory. Matthew's bass voice bounced around the room as he commanded Mallory into action. He finally came and collapsed his body. Seconds later, Mallory wrapped his arms around him, kissing him softly and whispering in his ears. When Matthew rose up and looked in his eyes, he realized that their secret had been revealed.

He turned toward Marek, licking his lips, then he spoke deeply, "Do you want to be next?"

Marek shook his head no.

Matthew growled, "... then get off my bloody bed."

Marek shot up and flew out of the room. As he rushed to the kitchen, he leaned over the sink and threw up. Mallory emerged from the bedroom wearing his navy terrycloth robe and handed Marek a towel.

Attempting to make light of the situation, he said with a smile, "Yeah, his sexy ass has the same effect on me." He teased him further, "Now don't let him see you do that ... that shit turns him on. That's a sign that you can be converted." He laughed.

Matthew emerged and Marek stepped behind the bar. "Who threw up in the sink?" Matthew asked looking at Mallory.

Mallory shook his head "I don't do that anymore."

Matthew looked at Marek with an intimidating face while he turned on the water in the sink to rinse it out. Marek was terrified. Matthew went to hand Marek a glass of water, and Marek pushed it out of his hands. Mallory laughed uncontrollably. He continued to tease Marek by grabbing and holding him down while Matthew walked toward him. "Get him!" he shouted.

Marek was outraged. He started screaming, "Get off me you stupid muthafucka."

Matthew stopped and then took a couple of steps back. "Emerald, what are you doing? Stop doing that, it's not funny." Matthew sat down.

Mallory let Marek go and he started punching Mallory. He tried to deflect Marek's punches but he was laughing too hard. Marek eventually stopped and looked at Matthew.

Matthew stared him down. "Are you going to hit me? I'll hit back."

"What in the fuck are you two doing? Hell I know what you're doing? Mallory, I thought you were... damn, I'm so confused." Marek shook his head.

"I know it looks bad." Mallory initiated an explanation. "But, why are you here?"

"Damn it, I forgot." Marek wanted to sit down but jumped up. "This is some fucked up shit, you know that?"

"Why Marek?" He forced him to sit and answer.

"Oh, Uncle M-Lee is in the hospital. He has stomach cancer."

Mallory was puzzled. It had been years since he interacted with parts of his family. He sat back trying to remember the people and events without rehashing the pain of his childhood. "Is he the angry one, or the one who cooked all the time?"

"The one who cooked all the time. We used to go to his house every summer. You would know these people if you showed up to the weekly family brunches."

"Whatever! We went every summer?"

"Yeah. Well maybe not you. You stopped going after that cake incident."

"What cake incident?" Matthew asked.

"I don't want to talk about that." Mallory's face turned pale.

"This muthafucka ate a whole chocolate cake."

"NO I DIDN'T," Mallory shouted and started shaking. Matthew grabbed him, trying to calm him down. "I don't think I can go see him."

"Mallory, he wants you there. It's your turn."

"Why? He asked for me?"

"Yeah, he's been waiting to see you ever since you got back."

"I don't know, Marek."

"Look. Come. The man is dying. It's terminal."

"I'll go with you if you want." Matthew wrapped his arm around Mallory's shoulder.

"I guess. Look, I know I was fucking with you, but we're trying to sort through this relationship, so can you keep it a secret?"

"Who the fuck I'm gonna tell? I ain't taking that ass whooping for nobody. Tell yourself. This shit is gonna to come back on you."

"Marek, this is not a phase. I'm not experimenting here."

"So you're gay?"

"No! Yes?" He looked at Matthew.

"Yes, Emerald. This is a gay relationship," Matthew confirmed.

"Look. It's complicated."

"I don't like complicated shit. Just don't fuck me and we cool." Marek stood up.

"I don't fuck my brothers."

Marek threw his hands up. "Who is this bitch?"

"Marek, it's complicated."

"Bye," Marek rushed out the door. "I'll see you at the hospital. You need to watch it. You keep lying to yourself and you will end up there...in the psych ward." Marek stormed out toward his black Jeep.

Mallory followed him out. "Hey what hospital?"

"He's in Hospice Austin."

"That bad?"

"Yeah. Hey is this serious with you and ..."

"Yes. I'm not that much of a freak. It's kinda hard for me, but I love him. He's it for me, Marek."

"Him and all the other women you fuck."

"No Marek. He's it. I haven't slept with a woman since the trip."

"What trip? Breckenridge? So that sissy ass noise I was hearing from your room was not the fucking TV? You were fucking in the room next to me? OH MY GOD! You two faggots!"

"Stop! Matty will hear you."

"I don't give a fuck about him hearing me! So you're telling me this muthafucka is so good that you lost all appetite for pussy."

"It's a struggle. I haven't been to the club or Molina's. I don't frequent the places where I can get tempted anymore."

"Shit! Just when I thought we can hang."

"Why do you think we can't hang?"

"I don't need you checking out men. Shit, you check out the wrong man and I'm fighting."

"I don't check out men. I'm not g..."

"Mallory, figure it out, fix your story and tell it to me later. I gotta go." Marek jumped back in his Jeep. "Go see him. He wants to talk to you."

Mallory went back into the house and saw Matthew waiting for him on the couch, so he found a safe distance spot and sat down.

"We knew this was going to get out, and I know that this is a little soon for you but...are you embarrassed to be with me?"

"No. I just don't want Malcolm having another excuse of..."

"Of what. Are you scared of what Dad would think?"

Mallory looked away.

"He'll be fine with this?"

"Maybe for you...he's never fine with anything I do."

"You and I have the same Dad, but different views about him. Why is that?"

"Maybe he loved your mother more, I don't know! Let's just drop this. I need to get ready."

"Every time I mention Dad you cringe like you're scared of him."

"I'm not scared of him!" Mallory jumped up in defense.

"He's an open-minded guy. I mean he was fine with me being gay. Maybe the brother thing will get him, but he'll accept us."

"He'll accept you. He has never accepted me. I was a cancer he couldn't get rid of." Mallory walked away. "Please, I gotta get ready."

"Emerald, I don't understand. Were you a bad kid?"

"A bad kid? I guess. I just don't remember doing the bad stuff." Mallory fought back tears forming in his eyes. "Look, I think I need to go see Uncle M-Lee."

"Emerald, talk to me. I want to understand more about this, and it's not going to buzz off just because you have someplace to go." He stood in front of him. "Like this whole chocolate cake, thing. You don't like chocolate." Mallory stood against the wall as if he was standing in front of a firing squad. Matthew could see Mallory's disposition changing drastically. "Talk to me ..."

"Chocolate was my favorite." He started wringing his hands and breathing erratically as he allowed the bad memory to flood his mind. "I wanted a piece of cake before dinner and I asked Uncle M-Lee. He didn't care. He cut a piece and we started eating it together ... but when Malcolm walked in, he was pissed." Mallory fought back the tears. "He grabbed the whole cake and shoved it down my throat. I couldn't breathe because I was inhaling cake." Mallory paused, closing his eyes.

Matthew saw his pain as he relived the abuse. "Look I don't need to hear the story now," he interrupted. "Let's just get ready." Matthew attempted to walk away but Mallory snatched his arm.

"NO! You wanted to hear the fucking story. You stand there and listen to the fucking story. Don't move until I say so." Mallory's roar frightened Matthew a bit. He had never heard that tone before.

Mallory continued. "I couldn't breathe. Uncle M-Lee tried to stop him but Malcolm slashed him across his face with a filet knife. He was screaming at me and Uncle M-Lee was bleeding." Mallory slid to the floor and then crawled in the corner. "Uncle M-Lee was bleeding. It was my fault. I should have waited. Dad said that it was my fault that I caused it and I was a waste. 'Look what you made me do you little bastard.' He kept saying ... and I couldn't move ... I couldn't breathe." Mallory rocked back and forth.

Matthew kneeled down beside him, but he was afraid to touch him. He vaguely remembered Mallory having one of these episodes in college, but it was alcohol and drug induced.

"He kept screaming 'you little bastard.' I couldn't breathe ... then I threw up. I couldn't hold it anymore. I just threw up." Mallory covered his mouth with both hands trying hard not to vomit on the floor. "... he made me." Mallory couldn't hold it in any longer; he vomited on the floor and on Matthew.

Matthew couldn't stay silent any longer. "Emerald, don't do this. Come on. Let's get up." He grabbed Mallory and attempted to pull him up, but Mallory jerked his arms back and started smearing the vomit over the floor.

"No I have to stay here. I threw up. I can't go until I clean this up."

"Peter can clean this up."

"I can't eat this Dad. Please, Dad. No." Mallory's hands began shaking as he smeared vomit on his arms and chest. Matthew grabbed for his arms again but Mallory starting fighting him. He sat back for a moment to regroup, and then he shuffled along side of him and grabbed him from behind.

"Emerald, Dad is not here. You don't have to eat this. I want you to take a shower." Matthew pulled him away from the mess. "Look at me. Matty wants you to take a shower. Dad is not here. It's just me ... only me."

"He'll come and get me. He always does."

"Not if I'm here, he won't. I'll protect you."

"Nobody protects me. They say they do. But they don't. Nobody cares." Mallory continued his rambling. "...I can't eat. I have to eat this before I can get up."

"I will protect you. He's not here. He won't come here, not as long as I'm here." Mallory looked up. "He'll never hurt you. Never! Your angel is here. Remember your angel? Nothing hurts me." Matthew finally lifted him up and hoisted him against the wall. "Look, we're not visiting any uncles today. I don't give a damn what they say. Let them come after me." He walked Mallory into the bedroom and sat him on the bed. He went into the bathroom and turned on the shower. He walked back to find Mallory standing at the door. "Let's take a shower together."

"Not my shower!" He shouted. "Not my shower."

CHAPTER TWO

Thirty-seven minutes passed and they were still sitting in the car. Matthew wanted desperately to tell Mallory that he could visit him later, but Mallory was adamant about visiting him today. Matthew watched several times as Mallory grabbed his keys, paused, then laid them back down. At one point, Mallory reached for the door latch, but his hand froze. Ten more minutes passed, Matthew couldn't take it anymore.

He patiently grabbed Mallory's hand, "Baby, take your time, but remember time is against him."

Mallory perked up a bit to open the car door this time, and slowly got out. He paused and attempted to retreat in the car, but Marek spotted him.

"Hey, you made it. He's waiting for you." Marek flung his arm across Mallory's shoulders and pulled him in.

As they walked into the hospital, Mallory felt wandering spirits surround him, giving him a strong sense of warmth and completeness. He couldn't understand where these feelings were stemming from, but he had an overwhelming urge to connect with them. Marek could feel and see the tension leave Mallory's body. Mallory eventually made it to the room to see everyone waiting for him. He took a couple more steps and noticed a frail man lying in a small hospital bed covered in an over-washed dingy white sheet and ratty looking blanket. Mallory barely recognized him. The last time he saw his uncle, he was a three hundred pound man who stood tall and strong.

Mallory managed to crack a smile as he slowly approached Uncle Murphy. "Hey Uncle M-Lee."

"Hey little pint. I guess I can't call you that anymore." He laughed then started choking.

Mallory fell to his aid. "You can call me whatever you want." Mallory searched hard for a suitable question to ask, since asking 'How are you doing' wasn't appropriate. "Do you need anything?"

"Yes, I need to speak with you alone."

Everyone slowly walked out of the room. Marek was the last to leave. He paused for a moment to make sure that Mallory was alright. Marek patted him on the shoulder. Mallory looked up and gave a reassuring nod. He returned his attention back to Uncle Murphy, grabbing his hand and stroking it softly. "We're alone now."

"You have grown to be a fine son."

"Thank you."

"I followed your success and I'm proud of you. You have turned out better than we expected. You're a true warrior."

"Warrior? You used to call me that all the time."

"You are a warrior. You're strong and determined. You're a survivor."

"I guess."

"I need to tell you some things, so listen very carefully." Mallory leaned in attentively. "Mallory, you need to join your brothers. It's very important."

Mallory fell back in disgust. "I can't believe that they would put you up to this on your death bed."

"Mallory, I'm serious. Join your brothers and take your position. You're the most important part of the group. It ends with you." He coughed again.

"I will."

"Are you still learning your languages?"

"Yes, I have mastered most all of them."

"Go back to the ancient books and learn the real history. Our family has been derailed and you need to get us back on track. Read the history in its language and teach it to the younger generation. Give them a better start than we gave you four."

"Okay?" he said confusingly.

"Follow no one. You have to be a loner. Never get too close. It will affect your judgment. That's what happened to your father." He coughed again. Mallory went to give him water but he wouldn't drink. "Mallory, love whoever you want, but don't get too close. Enjoy your life. Take every moment and enjoy it. There are no consequences, just regrets."

"Anything else?"

"Face your demon."

Mallory looked away.

"He's not as powerful as you think. You give up your power too quickly. Never give up your stance."

"Uncle M-Lee, he still scares me."

"I know, and just as you're afraid of him, he's more afraid of you. You're taking his position in the family and he must bow to you."

"Uncle M-Lee, Marc is taking his position."

"Don't be stupid, son! Marc can't take that position. It's your charge, your destiny."

Mallory was further confused because he thought Marc was the next president of the company. He decided to flow with the ramblings of an old dying man. Matthew walked back in to check on Mallory. Mallory looked up at him and flashed a reassuring smiled.

"Are you okay, baby?" Matthew asked.

"I'm fine. Are you ready to go?"

"Oh no, take your time. I wanted to see if you need anything. I was going to grab a bite. Want me to bring you something back?"

"Anything you bring me will be fine."

"Okay, hit my cell if you need anything." Mallory grabbed his hand and kissed it. Matthew patted his shoulder then walked out. Seconds later, Mallory realized that Uncle Murphy was still in the room. He couldn't think of what to say. He continued stroking his hand, attempting to ignore the situation.

"He's a handsome soul." Uncle Murphy said inquisitively.

"Do you know Matthew?"

"Yes, I do. He's one of Malcolm's. At least Malcolm says he is." Uncle Murphy said sarcastically. "I have a secret."

"What? I'm not his?" Mallory joked.

"Oh no! You two are cut from the same cloth." Uncle Murphy said proudly. Mallory's smile transformed to disgust. "Your father is a wonderful man."

"How can you say that? The little that I do remember about him is that he cheated on mom and he beat me. I know he killed some people."

"Mallory, are you judging?"

"No, these are facts."

"How are you looking at the picture?"

"Clearly. I'm still having nightmares."

"You need to proselyte."

"What does that have to do with anything?"

"Mallory, you're confusing an old man. Proselyte. Join your brothers. Shed your emotions and release this fear." He squirmed around to find a comfortable spot and grimaced.

"I'm confused." He shook his head. "Never mind. What was the secret?"

"I think someone has brought shame to our name."

Mallory shook his head again. "Who me? Because I'm sleeping with Matthew? I'm sick of this shit. Look, I love him. He means everything to me, alright. I'm trying to deal with the fact that we are brot ... half-brothers. But I love him and we're together. So, I bring shame to the family. This shit makes no sense to me."

"I didn't know that you were sleeping with him." Uncle Murphy said calmly. Mallory slapped his mouth hard. "That's not what I'm talking about. You have not proselyted, so it can't be you ... but you will have to set the chains of power correct. Find out who broke a ritual and rectify the situation."

"How am I supposed to do that?"

"You will know. Proselyte and it will come to you." Mallory absorbed the request. Uncle Murphy gathered enough strength to sit up in the bed. "Now why are you sleeping with your fucking brother?" He punched Mallory in his chest. "You couldn't find anyone else?"

"It's not like that. I didn't know we were brothers before all of this."

"What does father say about it?"

"Nothing!" He wanted to stick that answer, but he had to finish it. "Because he doesn't know," Uncle Murphy laughed so hard until he couldn't catch his breath. He began spitting up blood. "Please don't tell him," Mallory begged.

"Me tell him? I'm dying and I won't take that ass whooping."

"That's what Marek said."

"Marek knows? I heard of trying new things to replace your charge. But if he finds out, he's going to die. That's one for the history book." Mallory smiled, but he didn't understand the conversation. All the excitement quickly tired the old man; Uncle Murphy eventually slumped down in his bed.

"I'll leave you to get some rest."

"No Mallory? Where are you going?"

"I'm leaving. You need to rest." Mallory got up, but Uncle Murphy pulled him back on the bed.

"Mallory, what's wrong? Why are you acting this way?"

"What way? Concerned?"

"You want me to ask you?" He looked pitiful. "Please release me?" Mallory was completely oblivious to Uncle Murphy's request.

Marek came in. "Hey what's up?"

Mallory jumped up and sprinted toward Marek. "I'll be right back." He pushed Marek out of the room. "He wants me to release him. What am I supposed to do, sneak him out of here?"

"No. Release his soul."

"What in bloody hell are you talking about?"

Marek pushed him up against the wall. "I swear. That's why you shouldn't be fucking Matthew. You get screwed up."

"What does this have to do with Matty?" Marek pushed him against the wall again. "Why are you so angry with me?"

Marek retracted back to his corner. "You really don't know?" Mallory shook his head no. "Look I'll help you, but you have to take his soul. I'm not calling Dad for this, cuz he asked for you." He walked back in, but Mallory stayed against the wall. Marek stuck his head outside the door and shouted, "Bring yo' ass!"

Mallory slowly returned into the room looking very completely lost. "Have you ever command a soul?" Mallory shook his head. He walked over to Uncle Murphy. "Fuck, look. He doesn't know what he's doing. I guess he fucking forgot. So ... sit on the bed Mallory."

Uncle Murphy grabbed his hand. "Why didn't you just tell me you forgot?" Mallory hunched his shoulders. "That's okay. There are so many things to remember."

"Yeah, like if you're a faggot or not." They both looked up at Marek. "I know you told him. You talk so fucking loud, everybody heard you. If Marc or dad was out there ... damn!"

"Leave Marek, we'll be fine."

Marek stormed out.

"He needs to be careful with that temper. Someone will be calling for his soul soon." He turned back to Mallory. "Do you remember when we buried my wife?"

Mallory thought hard about his faded childhood memories. "Vaguely. She was in a glass coffin?"

"Yes, son. Remember the song?"

"I'll fly away?"

"Kinda. Remember the other words?"

Mallory closed his eyes and thought back to that time. He remembered Uncle Murphy and Aunt Sally fighting. Malcolm stormed in and slammed her against the wall. She never got up. He walked toward Uncle Murphy screaming something at him. Mallory shook his head no.

Uncle Murphy stroked his hand softly. "Think Mallory. The glass coffin."

Mallory remembered hiding in the corner watching Malcolm place her lifeless body into a glass coffin chanting words over her. He remembered Malcolm singing louder and louder. He closed his eyes to focus on Malcolm's lips, trying to decipher the words. He recalled Malcolm grabbing him and making him kneel before the coffin. Mallory jumped and his eyes flew open.

"Malcolm made me sing that song. Yes, I remember." That was one of the few times he and Malcolm did anything that didn't involve abuse. Mallory took a deep breath and began singing the words. "One fine morning when this life is over, I'll fly away." The room grew dark, the doors flew open, and windows shattered. The billowy shadow that haunted Mallory for some time returned through a broken window and hovered over the bed. It encircled Mallory as he began his transformation. His skin turned ice cold and his eyes glared icy blue. His voice grew dark and loud, sending cracks up the wall to the ceiling. "When I die Hallelujah by and by, I'll fly way." Mallory started singing the reverse of the mantra in the same melody. Uncle Murphy laid back and closed his eyes. His body jumped as Mallory stood over him with his arms stretched wide. A stream of spirits rushed in and encircled Mallory.

Mallory was deep in transformation and didn't notice Matthew slipping into the room. Matthew tiptoed to the other side when Mallory flashed his eyes open. He looked straight through Matthew as if he were not there. Matthew noticed that Mallory's eyes were icy blue. His ears began ringing and he felt dizzy and sick. He eventually collapsed on the floor knocking down the food tray. Marek strolled by and noticed Matthew seizing on the floor. He quickly ran into the room and dragged him out. Mallory raised his arms to the ceiling and commanded Uncle Murphy's spirit to be lifted out of his body and joined with the rest of the spirit circle. Mallory emptied his lungs and inhaled all the spirits. The room flashed pitch black and cold, and then went silent.

Marek finally plopped Matthew on a chair. He was out of it as his body ached with unimaginable pain. He started sliding out of the chair, but Marek pulled him up. When Marc walked out of the elevator, he noticed Marek struggling with Matthew. He quickly grabbed Matthew's arm, helping him back in the chair.

"Is Mallory in there?" Marc said, pulling Matthew up in the chair.

"Yeah, he's almost finished. You know he forgot how to do it?"

"That doesn't make sense. As many times as he got beat because he kept singing the song and you know he almost commanded Dad's soul."

"I think that was the worst ass whooping ever."

"Yeah it was," he looked down at Matthew. "What's wrong with him?"

"Oh this son of a bitch here walked in when Mallory was calling for Uncle M-Lee? Bitch trying to kill his damn self."

Marc laughed. "You stupid ass. That shit hurts doesn't it?" He tossed Matthew's head around.

Matthew managed to move Marc from his head. "Commanding his soul?"

"Yeah, Death has to do that." Marc said.

"Death?" Matthew tried to follow the conversation but his head was splitting with pain, so he retreated to tend to himself.

"Aunt Steph will be coming soon, so we need to start gathering. Hey, get up." Marc snatched Matthew's arm, "I'll take you outside to get some air. Marek, you check on Mallory. You get him some boiling water. You know he's gonna need it. I'm glad I'm not him."

Mallory walked toward a chair and sat down quietly. He looked over at his uncle, who appeared to be fast asleep. He was so confused. He commanded a soul. Marek said he was terminal. Maybe that was his favorite song and he just wanted to hear it.

Maybe, he just wanted to say his last good-byes to everyone personally.

"I didn't command a soul." With every waking thought, sharp chills ran down his body.

Marek finally return to the room and sat with him. "Are you okay?" He examined his brother, who possessed no emotions.

"I'm cold." He made no eye contact and frost escaped his breath.

"I got you some water." Marek said as he gently handed him the water. Mallory brought the cup to his lips. But before he could drink, the water turned to ice. So he dropped the cup.

"I'm cold Marek."

"Shit." Marek snatched the blanket from the bed and quickly wrapped it around Mallory, who was shivering uncontrollably. "Shit!" Marek ran out of the room and returned with a coffeepot of boiling water. He held Mallory's head back and poured it down his throat. Mallory calmed down a bit but he was still shivering. Marek sat on floor with him, holding him tight and rocking him. "I'm so fucking glad that I'm not you. I can't go through this shit."

"What's happening?"

"You'll be alright. Don't think about it. Let's talk about something."

Mallory noticed Uncle Murphy's monitors were still showing signs of life. "Is he still alive?"

"Yeah, his soul is released but his body has to shut down. We didn't want his soul trapped in a dead body."

"Why?"

"Why are acting like you don't know this shit?"

"I don't."

"Look, I don't know what you need to do but this mental block shit is for the birds."

"Marek, I'm scared."

"You know what? You need to stop saying that you're fucking scared. Never say that damn word again. Never admit it, even if you're scared shitless. You're a fucking Haulm, do you hear me?"

Mallory nodded.

"Look, I'm here for you. I locked the door so we can get through this, but Mallory I can't be with you all the time."

Mallory nodded.

"How are you feeling?"

"I'm still cold but I'm okay. Do you think I brought shame to the family because of Matthew?"

"Because of the gay shit? You can only bring shame if it breaks rituals. You haven't proselyted, yet. Besides, you ain't the only gay one in the family." Marek mimicked quotation marks with his fingers. "Aunt Steph? Uncle M-Lee's friend."

"Aunt Steph? I thought she was a woman ... an ugly woman."

"You're so stupid." He laughed.

"I didn't know she was a man. Wasn't that his wife's sister ... or brother?"

"Yep. I guess getting stuck in the ass is a Haulm tradition too."

"It's not like that."

"How is it then? I don't think you know."

Mallory ignored the comment. The warmth began slowly creeping back in his body. "Aunt Steph's a man. I hope I don't look like that."

"You won't. You two are the gay muthafuckas women hate."

"Hate?"

"Yeah, there are some faggots out there that the woman would say take his short bald small dick ass ... but you two piss them off. I mean, face it. We are the Fucking Haulm brothers. We are the Adonis clan. We command all. Those sissies in Hollywood idolize us."

Mallory laughed.

"Come now, Godiva chocolate ain't got nothing on our flavors. We come in a range of vanilla to the deepest darkest special chocolate that the world has every produced. Can I get a witness?"

"Amen."

"You can have fifteen minutes or fifteen days. It's what you can handle." Marek continued preaching. "We can have an island of fucking cream of the crop women and never have to fuck the same one at least for six months."

"I guess."

"And you want to bump booties with your brother. I'd be a pissed bitch. I would walk up to you and bitch slap your ass."

"But I'm happy."

"Are you really happy...are you hiding behind him?" Marek asked.

He paused. "I'm happy."

"Okay. I have nothing more to say. I just think you're hiding behind him and he's fucking with your proselytization."

"I'm going to proselyte, once someone tells me what that means. He's not going to stand in the way of that."

"Are you sure? I mean. I like the guy. But if he gets in the way, he has to be eliminated. We can't take any chances."

"He's not going to get in the way. Wha-wha-what do you mean eliminated?"

"You know. Set aside. On ice. Just be careful. Don't let him get in your way. Figure this out. Don't make any announcement until you figured this out and only after you proselyte. And please, don't tell Dad. We do not need him wigging out. I can't handle visiting the psych ward again."

"You think he would be ashamed?" Mallory rocked back and forward to calm his fears.

"Ashamed? You don't want to piss off Dad. How can I say this nicely ... he's crazy!"

Everyone gathered in the room and waited for Uncle Murphy to die. When he finally passed away, Aunt Steph began sobbing uncontrollably. Matthew consoled him, while Mallory sat in the corner trying to rehash the events, but he was overwhelmed with grief. Mallory's few fond memories of his childhood passed away. He looked at Aunt Steph and felt his terrible loss. He couldn't image losing Matthew. He walked to him and placed his hand gently on his shoulder and Aunt Steph looked up.

Mallory said softly, "We're going to take you home." Aunt Steph nodded and laid his head back on Matthew's chest. Mallory left the room and Matthew jumped up to him follow him. "Hey, Aunt Steph needs to sign some release forms. I was thinking, why don't you go the store and —"

"You want me to go to a store?

"You're a big boy. Just pull out your little credit card and they'll give you anything you want."

"Why can't I call Peter?" Before Mallory could finish his sentence, Matthew shot hate darts through his eyes. "Go to a store and get something for dinner?"

"Yeah. Do you think we need to spend the night?"

Mallory hunched his shoulders.

"Get breakfast too, I guess."

Marek walked up. "What's up?"

"I'm sending Emerald to the store to get something for dinner. I think we should cook for him. He doesn't need to be alone tonight."

"Cool. I'm coming. I heard about your little dishes. You English people think you can cook."

"Shit it ain't nothing but a thang muthafucka, bring your belly." Matthew laughed at his failed attempt to speak Ebonics.

Marek rolled his eyes. "I'm there. Let me go tell Jean and them."

"Oh, is this going to be a family thing?" Matthew worried about Mallory's mood swings.

"I guess so," Mallory answered.

"Are you going to be okay with that?"

"I'll be okay, as long as I have my angel there." Mallory smiled softly.

"Damn it! I don't need to hear the freaky shit. I'm just coming to eat," Marek said.

Matthew turned around and Mallory noticed a bruise on his forehead. "What happened?"

"I don't know. I walked in the room to see if you were okay. I can't remember anything after that. It looks worse than it feels."

Mallory gently grabbed his head and lowered it down to kiss it. "Here let me kiss it and make it feel better."

"If you want me to feel better, I have another head you can kiss." He bit his lip.

"That's the shit I'm talking about. Just bitch slap the both of you." Marek stormed off. Matthew and Mallory smiled at each other and Mallory snuck a peck. He whispered 'I love you' then walked away trying to catch up with Marek. Matthew waited for Aunt Steph to finish with the hospice administrators.

𝕸

Mallory watched the hustle and bustle of the family once everyone arrived at Aunt Steph's house. Although witnessing his family fuss and laugh over spirits and food made Mallory happy, he couldn't help feel out of place. It was as if he was an extra in a movie. He found a safe haven in the kitchen and admired the activity from a distance. In the midst of all the family togetherness, Mallory baked a chocolate cake, a favorite activity he shared with Uncle Murphy. Matthew noticed that he wasn't around with the rest of the family, so he went to search for him. As he walked in the kitchen, he saw Mallory icing very carefully with such great pride.

"What are you doing?"

Mallory stopped. "I don't know. Everyone was talking and laughing and I was compelled to bake this cake."

"Okay, don't you think you need to step away from the cake? I don't think we need an episode like this morning."

"I think I'll be okay."

Marek stumbled in the kitchen and bellowed intoxicatingly, "What are you two queer eyes doing?"

Matthew turned around and noticed Malcolm standing behind Marek with a highball glass in his hand. He prowled toward Mallory as if he was in attack mode, peering over Mallory's shoulder. Mallory stood frozen as he felt the hot breath of anger hit the back of his neck. He remembered Uncle Murphy saying to face his demon, but he wasn't ready.

"What are we doing, son?" Malcolm asked darkly but Mallory didn't speak. Malcolm took the knife from his hand then cut the cake. Mallory was pissed, but fear overcame him and he couldn't react. "I thought we didn't eat chocolate cake anymore," Malcolm teased him.

Mallory was speechless.

His brothers knew this was a test, and they couldn't afford to help him. Mallory finally managed to look into Malcolm's eyes. They were ice cold and hollow.

Malcolm picked up a piece of cake and held it out for Mallory. "Eat the cake, son."

He was petrified. Images of him throwing up and having to eat his vomit sickened him more. He tried to sense if Matthew was around him but he couldn't feel his presence because of the overpowering presence of Malcolm's anger. He held back the tears and tried to keep eye contact with Malcolm but he blinked and a tear fell.

At that moment, Matthew grabbed the cake and ate it. "Thanks Dad." He walked toward the refrigerator and opened it. "Damn this cake is moist. I need milk." Matthew decided since Marek confirmed to the family that he was gay, he would play a flaming role. He walked back over to Mallory. "Wanna piece of cake, baby?" He took another bite and kissed Mallory, placing it in his mouth.

"Now that's how you eat cake," Aunt Steph shouted.

Everybody else grimaced. Malcolm was steaming pissed. This was a clear sign to Marek that Mallory was hiding behind Matthew. He couldn't face Malcolm just yet.

Matthew broke his kiss and frowned up at Malcolm. Everyone resumed talking and Mallory quickly left the kitchen bringing the cake to the table.

Malcolm cornered Matthew by grabbing his arm. "Nice stunt!" Malcolm shouted. "Who do you think you are, Angelina

Jolie? Don't make it a habit of kissing Mallory like that. I don't need him to become like —"

"Like what, Dad! You're great to me and I love you. I don't know what it's about Mallory you don't like. But don't fuck with him! That's my baby ... brother and I'm going to protect him even if that means hurting you."

"You think you can take me on," Malcolm growled.

"I don't fear you like the others," Matthew matched his anger. "All giants fall!"

"That's stupid on your part." He grabbed his arms tightly and screamed, "I have accepted you as a faggot, but you will not turn my son into one." Malcolm stormed off.

Everyone sat back at the table and settled down to eat. Mallory tried to eat but he could feel Malcolm's anger choking him. He sat back and resorted to a liquid dinner of white wine. Aunt Steph decided to break the eerie mood by suggesting that everyone say something they remembered about Uncle Murphy. Mallory didn't have many good memories. His childhood was a sad case but he tried coming up with a happy memory. Matthew made it worse by saying that he really didn't know Uncle Murphy and was going to let Mallory come up with one for him. Mallory shook his head and downed his third glass of wine.

"Well. Damn. Uncle M-Lee. What can I tell you about Uncle M-Lee?" he paused and then poured another glass of wine. "He taught me how to make a chocolate cake." Everyone was silent. "Um, he taught me how to cook. He was a great cook." Mallory allowed his mind to wander back to those painful times. He remembered that Uncle Murphy wanted to be a singer. He always enlisted Mallory and the brothers to be his backup singers. "Ah ... he wanted to create his own group. Remember? We used to sing ... what's that bloody song? Cupid! We were the Mini Tops, remember?"

Marek bellowed. "Ah shit! Yeah! I remember that! We had a dance routine and everything."

"He even created outfits for us," Mallory laughed.

Aunt Steph walked over to the stereo and found the CD. "He was listening to this mess before he got sick this last time."

Mallory got up and grabbed Marek. "Come on, sing it with me."

"I only know the chorus. I was the dancer, remember?" Marek announced.

"I think I know the words. He played that damn song so much that the tape melted." Marc said.

"Hell yeah. He cried that whole day." Marek turned around. "Oh don't think you're getting out of this. Get your ass up, Marc."

"Nawh, we got bass over here." He pointed at Matthew.

"Ah no thank you... I don't know the dance routines."

"We don't either. Get up." Marek replied.

"Come sing with me, baby." Mallory mouthed seductively to Matthew. He couldn't resist Mallory's request. They all got in place, Marek putting Mallory in the middle. The song came on and they finally got in the groove. Marc placed Matthew in front of him so he could accompany Mallory in their makeshift skit. As he sang the words, he heard Matthew's voice.

With the mixture of wine and Matthew's voice, Mallory was getting aroused. Matthew's voice always gave him the shivers. He periodically turned and serenaded Matthew then deflected the affections by singing and teasing Marek. He finally grabbed Aunt Steph's hand and serenaded him. Everyone was enjoying the show. They finally made their finish and bowed for their applause.

"Mallory, you look like you got a group there," Uncle Myron joked and they all laughed.

"Look, I know this is Uncle M-Lee's night. But you got a song too. Marek, who was that wife who left him?"

"Now that's grown folks' business," Myron said.

"Have you not recognized that I AM grown," Mallory said.

"Ruby Lee," Marek shouted.

"Ruby Lee. Boy, now she was mean."

"He probably cheated on her." Marek joked.

"Marek!" everyone shouted.

"Shit, he probably did. I cheated on my wife." They laughed.

"He's paying for that shit," Jean added sharply, rolling her eyes.

"I think we are evenly matched!" Marek shot his eyes at Jean then at Marc.

"What was the damn song? Remember you would drink that Thunderbird." Mallory searched in his mind to remember the chorus.

"I can't remember. But it had a big red girl in it," Marc added.

"When She was My Girl?" Matthew asked.

"Yeah!" They all screamed.

"I got that song too." Aunt Steph jumped up and ran back to the stereo.

The boys sat back at the table. Uncle Myron decided he would sing his own song. The boys sang backup for him. Mallory grabbed Matthew's hand secretly under the table as they both sang the bass part together. Although they were singing backup, they helped Uncle Myron sing their favorite part.

"The big red girl is gone!"

Mallory saw Malcolm's anger melt a little and he was even enjoying the song. He wanted to maintain a level of no confrontation, but that feeling ended when Matthew asked Malcolm what his favorite song was.

"Who's Making Love to Your Ole Lady?" Aunt Steph snickered. Uncle Mal coughed and his face went pale. He made no eye contact with anyone. Mallory saw everyone's blank expression except Malcolm, whose face was repainted with pure anger.

"Is that why I'm named after you?" Mallory asked.

"No!" Uncle Mallory quickly dispelled loudly.

Matthew broke the silence by laughing. "Will that still make us brothers?"

Mallory looked from the corner of his eye. "No cousins ... half cousins. I can do cousins." They both laughed at their inside joke.

"Oh two faggots! That's some nasty shit." Marek shrugged but Mallory grabbed him and shook him until he finally cracked a smile.

Mallory resolved his laughter when he felt the heavy tension grow between the two men. With each breath Malcolm took, his anger brewed. Mallory thought of the rumors that he heard about his birth. He was born early. Malcolm was away to witness the birth of Matthew, so Uncle Mal took his mom to the hospital. He studied them for a long time and wondered if he was the reason for the rift between them.

Matthew broke Mallory's stare by sneaking a kiss on the cheek. "Help me clean the table."

He started picking up dishes from the table. As he walked into the kitchen, he looked back at the two men. Malcolm peered down at Uncle Mal, daring him to look up. Uncle Mal eventually left the table, leaving Malcolm sitting alone. As he looked on, Malcolm's expression turned from anger to pain. Mallory quietly placed the dishes in the sink, keeping watch. He sensed that someone was behind him, but he didn't fear the presence because Malcolm was in his sight.

A hand touched his shoulder and the voice said, "He can be broken down. This might be a good time for you to speak with him."

CHAPTER THREE

Matthew spent many late nights at Haulm Industries reassigning and delegating duties in his department. He was preparing to leave for his first trip to Jerusalem to meet his team. Mallory was away on business, and Matthew knew he wasn't going to be home for a while, so Matthew decided to pull an all-nighter. He settled in his office, turning the lights down low and working by only the lamp on his desk. He borrowed a bottle of Hennessey and a Ray Charles CD from Malcolm's office. After Matthew had been there awhile, he received a call from Mallory. They exchanged a few flirtatious comments. Mallory told him, since he was staying in the office all night, he would meet him there.

Mallory strolled in a couple of hours earlier than expected. Since the first-class family trip to Breckenridge was a fiasco, he decided to buy a leer jet. After being able to rush home or leave when he desired, he wondered why he hadn't thought of buying a jet sooner. As he walked down the hall of the sixth floor, he noticed that all the lights were off except for one in the corner. As he moved closer, he heard Ray Charles blaring in the air. He reached the door and saw Matthew drinking and singing to himself. He crept in slowly, taking off his shoes and coat. He loosened his tie and waited for Matthew to notice him. Matthew finally looked up and a smile exploded on his face.

Mallory screamed out the stanza, "BABY! BABY! BABY! OH BABY! Do I love you?" He fell to his knees and crawled toward Matthew, stripping off his clothes. "Tease me ... squeeze me ...

leave me ... ah don't leave me!" He stood up and allowed his pants to fall to the floor. "Take my hand! I don't need ... no other man now!" He continued his screaming and sauntered over to his hot lover.

Matthew rolled out behind the cherry wooden desk, grooving and enjoying his strip tease.

"Because nighttime is the right time ..." Mallory straddled him in the seat. "To be with the one you love now!" Mallory finally kissed Matthew.

He lifted Mallory from the chair and dropped him on the desk. Mallory fell back on the desk, allowing Matthew to remove his boxer briefs. Matthew's tongue glided up his inner thigh. Mallory pushed himself up to allow Matthew to climb on top of the desk. As Matthew enveloped his throbbing shaft, Mallory bit his tongue. He tried concentrating on undressing Matthew, but Matthew's deep throat maneuvers were getting the best of Mallory.

Ray Charles finally stopped singing and Mallory came. Before he could take a breath, Matthew rushed inside him. Moans filled the room. Matthew came and collapsed on Mallory's body. Moments later, they heard a thump.

"What was that?" Mallory asked.

"I don't know," Matthew answered exhaustedly.

"Nobody's coming here, right?"

"No. It's too late. Dad's out of town and not due back until the day after tomorrow. Your brothers wouldn't be here this late," Matthew rose up and noticed a body lying outside the door. "Oh shit!"

"What?" Mallory looked over and noticed his father lying lifeless on the floor. "Oooh, get up, get up." They both rushed up but then stood frozen behind the desk. Matthew grabbed his pants and convinced himself to walk over to see if Malcolm was still breathing. He slowly leaned down when Malcolm grabbed his neck. Although it was a weak grasp, it scared him. He managed to remove his hand. "He's breathing. Call 911."

Mallory stood frozen. The last time Malcolm was lying on the floor, he almost died. When Mallory was little, he ran through the house singing the death chant so loudly that it commanded Malcolm's soul. He heard the same thump as tonight. He remembered walking over to Malcolm's body. As he stood over the gigantic lifeless body, Malcolm jumped up and grabbed him, slamming him up against the wall.

"Emerald, come here."

"No! No, I can't."

"Emerald. EMERALD!" Matthew shouted. Mallory took baby steps toward Matthew, making sure Malcolm couldn't get up. "Look, I think he's going to be okay. I have to finish putting my clothes on. Sit with him."

"No! No! I can't." Mallory started walking backward.

"Emerald, what's wrong?"

"He'll crush me. I'll die this time. No one will save me."

"Emerald, I think he's having a heart attack. Come here."

"No. I'll call 911 then I'll call Marek." He turned and walked back toward the desk. Without taking his eyes off his father, Mallory fumbled with the phone. "Yes, I'm at Haulm Industries. There is a person having a heart attack." He paused. "Yes ... that's the address. It's ... my dad, Malcolm Haulm."

He remembered Malcolm making the same phone calls. It seemed to take forever for the emergency crew to arrive, as Mallory lay lifeless on the cold ground. He remembered choking on blood that collected in his throat and Malcolm bending over him to turn his body over. "You're not dying on me you, little bastard."

"Emerald, Stay here and I'll go down for security."

"No. I'll do it." Mallory walked fiercely toward the door then stopped short of reaching Malcolm's body. He fixed his eyes on Malcolm. He carefully stepped over him while watching for any signs of life. When Malcolm opened his eyes, Mallory fell back, landing on the ground. He laid there frozen, waiting for Malcolm to rise up but he didn't.

Get up. Get up, Mallory. Get up. He finally stood up and ran toward the elevators. He stormed out of the elevator and rushed to notify the security desk that his father was sick and the emergency crew was coming. Then he disappeared in a corner. He needed to call Marek.

"Who dis?"

"Marek, it's me." Mallory said in a quivering voice.

"What! Do you know how fucking late it is?" Marek shouted. Mallory heard a voice in the distance and Marek rudely answered, "No bitch! This is not my wife so shut up."

"Are you busy?"

"What the fuck do you want?"

"It's Dad." There was a long silence.

"You said Dad?" He changed his tone.

"Malcolm. It's Malcolm. He had a heart attack, I think."

"When?"

"Tonight. I'm waiting for the emergency crew to get here."

"To get where?"

He paused. He had no reason to be at Haulm Industries that late. "Look they're here. I'll call you and tell you where they're taking him."

"Mallory, where are you?"

He couldn't answer that question so he hung up. He saw Matthew walking down with Malcolm on the stretcher. He slowly walked up and noticed that Malcolm was awake.

"Hey, Emerald. They said he'll be okay. He's stabilized. They're taking him to H & H Mercy Hospital. He's going to be okay. Do you wanna ride with him, or do you want me to go?"

Mallory couldn't decide.

"Emerald. Do I need to call one for you? You look sick."

Mallory glanced over at Malcolm and their eyes locked. He had the same expression as that day; it was the last expression Mallory remembered before he blacked out. He took several steps back and then threw up.

"Emerald. Don't do this now. Shit. Don't do this now."

His eyes connected with Matthew's eyes. "He's going to crush me." Mallory rushed out the building and ran toward his car. He jumped in locking the doors and rocked himself until he saw the flashing lights of the ambulance disappear in the night. He decided to follow it. As he switched lanes, the cell phone rang. It was Marek.

"He's going to H & H Mercy Hospital. Where are you?"

"Down the street from there. Are you okay?" Marek said as he fumbled with the keys.

"Yeah. I'm just scar — worried about him."

"I'll meet you there."

Mallory finally made it to the hospital. He walked through the hospital's emergency doors and passed by the check-in counter. He wandered past the waiting room and emergency rooms until he reached a fork in the corridor. He started feeling that warmth and completeness he experienced at the hospice center. He aimlessly walked through different segments of the hospital, not particularly looking for Malcolm. Not reading the designated signs, he reached the oncology department. He strolled through several rooms noticing people in pain, screaming and moaning. He walked in one room and saw a spirit floating. It stopped and began floating toward Mallory. He turned around and ran out. He hastily tried to backtrack his way to the emergency room. When he turned a corner, he ran into Marek.

"Hey. I just got here. Where is he?"

"I don't know. I'm still looking for him." Mallory lied. "Did you call Marc?"

"Yeah, he's on his way." Marek turned around and followed the signs toward the emergency room. Mallory walked closely behind Marek. He saw many spirits floating around and following him. He wanted to tell Marek but he was preoccupied with finding Malcolm. As they backtracked to the emergency waiting room, Matthew walked up and got their attention.

"He's over here. He's checked in and they got him a room," Matthew said.

"Cool. Is he okay?" Marek asked.

"Yeah, they said it was very mild, but they're keeping him for observation."

"Cool, cool." Marek paused and looked at Matthew. "So, you checked him in?" Marek asked suspiciously.

"Yeah, I rode with him." Matthew answered.

"Where were you?" Marek asked.

"At the office," Matthew answered calmly.

Marek looked at Mallory but he avoided any eye contact. "Was Mallory there?"

"Yeah."

"What were you doing there, this late? I thought you were on a business trip," Marek's suspicions grew. Mallory saw Marek rationalizing the events in his mind. He quickly turned around and tried tuning out the conversation.

"He was helping with something ... work related," Matthew tried desperately to defuse the suspicion but Mallory's behavior was not helping.

"What were you doing there?" Marek ignored Matthew's lie.

"That's none of your business," Matthew answered coldly.

"I didn't ask your faggot ass." Marek turned to Mallory, standing confrontationally in his personal space. "I'm talking to this faggot ass."

Matthew pushed Marek away and stood between the two. "You got one more time to call me or him a fucking faggot. You'll be in a bed next to Dad."

"Why were you there, Mallory?" Marek shouted through Matthew as if he were invisible.

"I was just there helping," Mallory voice cracked.

"I'm supposed to believe that your muthafuckin' ass was just there, and Dad was so fucking happy that he had a got damn heart attack?"

Mallory couldn't answer nor could he look into Marek's eyes.

"Look at me bitch!" Marek shouted. Mallory finally raised his head. "Why were you there? What were you doing?"

"I really don't think that is any of your fucking business." Matthew charged at Marek.

"Step off, Matthew. This is brothers' business."

"Who in the hell do you think you are?" Matthew posted Marek against the wall. Mallory tried restraining him and Marek pushed them both off.

The nurse walked up looking for one of the family members. "Matthew Haulm. Is Matthew Haulm here?"

He looked around and raised his hand.

"Your father is asking for you."

"This shit's not finished." Matthew pushed him again and then stormed off to Malcolm's room.

"Tell me Mallory? And please don't tell me you told Dad. Tell me something, Mallory. Speak fucker." He posted Mallory against the wall. "Speak muthafucka!"

"Okay. I was hanging out with Matthew waiting for him to finish working." Mallory tried to sound convincing but his voice kept cracking.

"Try again."

Mallory took a deep breath. He knew Marek already knew the story by the guilty expression on his face. "He caught us."

"Son of a bitch! You stupid muthafucka! Didn't I tell you to play this shit cool? Didn't I tell you not to let Dad find out? Didn't I? You fucked up, Mallory. Do you ever stop to think about the shit you do, or do you just do it to piss people off?"

"No. I didn't mean to ..."

"To do what? Kill him? Your ass won't proselyte. What the fuck are we supposed to do if he dies? Do you think about that shit?"

"I don't want him to die."

"Really bitch? You don't want him to die but you would do some shit like this that nearly kills him and you won't take his position. You need to choose a side, bitch. You can't have it both ways."

"I don't understand."

"YOU'RE PISSING ME OFF WITH THIS MENTAL BLOCK SHIT!" He slammed both his fists against the wall on each side of Mallory.

"I don't have a mental block. I honestly don't know."

"I'm through with you. You're going to tell Marc. I'm not doing this shit no more. I'm not protecting you no more."

"No Marek, I can't tell him."

"You have two fucking options. You go in there and finish the fucking job on Dad or you fucking tell Marc before Dad does."

Marc finally reached the hospital. He saw Marek and Mallory in the corner talking. He strolled over and gently put his arm around Mallory's shoulders. Mallory couldn't look in his eyes.

"Hey. How is he doing?" Marc said calmly.

"Fine ..." Mallory's voice cracked. "They said that it was a mild one."

"Hey, it's okay." Marc hugged him. "He's strong. He's going to pull through. I keep telling him to take care of himself and stop mixing his meds with alcohol." He grabbed Mallory's face. "He works so hard and he puts a lot of pressure on himself to perform. I don't know how he travels back and forward to New York with his company. I don't understand why you two don't join your financial companies together, but that's another story." He tossed his face from side to side. "He'll be fine. Don't worry ... He's his own worst critic but he'll be okay. Just think positive." Marc hugged him. "You don't worry about a thing. You just get ready for the proselytization, okay? We're well on our way to running things."

Mallory nodded.

"He was at the office?"

"Yeah, he was at the fucking office!" Marek announced loudly.

"I'm glad that you were there," Marc said. Mallory gave a half-grin but he cringed when he saw the explosions going off in Marek's eyes. "Look, I'm going to check on him. I'll stay tonight. You go home and get some rest. Okay? Don't worry, he'll be fine."

Mallory nodded.

When Marc walked off, Marek threw Mallory against the wall again. "YOU ARE A BITCH! I can't believe that you're just going to stand there and let that man give you props. You like to play bitch moves, don't you? You think that we didn't see that bitch move with the cake. Matthew can't protect you when it's time."

"I can protect myself."

"Against who bitch? You can't stand up for anything. You're hiding like a little bitch."

"Stop calling me that."

"What the fuck am I supposed to call you? A fucking pussy! Pussy is stronger than you, Mallory! I had so much respect for you when you first came back. I mean you stood for something. You were about something. You had your shit together. Now, you're worse than a pussy. What is going on? Is it Matthew?"

"No! People think I'm supposed to be something great but nobody will tell me what that is!"

Marek glared at him. "I'm going to check on Dad. If I keep talking to you, you'll be in the morgue." Marek stormed off leaving Mallory standing in the corner like a hurt child.

Mallory slowly walked toward to the garage. He opened his car door and crawled in. He reclined his seat and tried hard to erase the night's events from his mind, but they blasted so loudly that the screams were hurting his ears. He reached in his compartment and found a full bottle of Absolut Vodka. He nursed the bottle until he fell asleep.

"You have to take your position. We need you. You're weak. You're a needed force in this family. Fucking faggot. It ends with you. You're hiding behind that bitch. We need you. We need you. We really need you."

Mallory's restless sleep was disturbed, when he felt a buzzing sensation in his chest. He patted his chest to find that it was his cell phone vibrating in his coat pocket. He flipped the phone open to see that he missed forty-seven calls. There were many from Matthew and home, which were still Matthew, a couple from Marek and one from Brielle.

That's the last thing I need. He looked over and saw the empty bottle of vodka and an open bottle of aspirin. *Damn, what a party? And I'm still here.* He looked out the window and noticed that he never left the hospital. Thinking back to the night, he realized that he never went to see Malcolm.

He entered the hospital slowly and those feelings of warmth and completeness filled his heart again, but this time they frustrated him. He quickly dismissed his frustration and searched for his father's name on the door. *M. Haulm.* He touched the door and his heart sank. He cracked the door open to peek in. No one was there. He stepped in and spotted Malcolm sleeping. He turned to walk out but he heard a faint voice calling him.

"Mallory?" Malcolm whispered.

Mallory answered. "Yes, sir?"

"Come in. I'm not asleep."

He turned back around and slowly walked in toward Malcolm. He remembered those times he was in the hospital bed and Malcolm would walk toward him, how frightened and helpless he felt. He still felt helpless, although he was the one walking toward the bed.

"Sit."

He found a chair in the corner. He didn't want to move the chair because it was a safe distance from Malcolm's reach, but he scooted the chair closer to the bed. There was no safe distance if Malcolm wanted to get him. "Sir?" He tried to go over the appropriate questions for the situation. "How are you feeling?"

"I've had better days."

Mallory couldn't respond to that answer. "I spoke with the doctors. They said you'll be fine. You'll be out of here in a couple days. They really urge you to stop mixing your meds with liquor."

Malcolm nodded.

Mallory wanted to shout, *Fucking hit me and get this over with. I'm in agony over this silence.* He finally made eye contact with Malcolm. "Dad? I'm sorry. I-I I didn't mean—"

"Mean what? Being a homosexual or me finding out?"

"I didn't mean to hurt you."

"Hurt me, Mallory? How?"

Mallory realized that the physical abuse was tolerable. At least he could tune out the hitting and think about something else. Answering questions under this pressure was more brutal. "I don't know. I mean I don't regret what I was doing. I-I love Matthew. I love him. I-I guess I just didn't want you to find out that way."

"Well, I guess if you were a man, you would have come and told me."

There was a long silence. Mallory was petrified, with mixed emotions of guilt and anguish. "Dad, I'm sorry."

"Yes you are. But if you wanna lead your life that way, so be it. I would have never thought that my son would be so pitiful and disgusting."

Mallory's body shuddered with the explosion. "I'm pitiful? Right," he paused. "But if Uncle M-Lee is right, you're pitiful too. Everyone keeps saying that we're bloody twins, cut from the same cloth. So, I guess that I'm pitiful fruit from a pitiful tree."

"You're no son of mine."

"I hope the fuck not!" He shouted. "I would never want you to be my father. I wouldn't wish that on any of my enemies." He stood up. "I hope you feel better. I have a man to go home to who loves me. I don't think you have ever experienced someone loving you." Mallory shoved the chair back in the corner and prepared to walk out.

"So you're choosing him. He didn't choose you, you know. He'll never choose you. You'll never be happy with him. He'll leave you like he did before." Malcolm sat up a bit and tried mustering any strength he had to breakdown Mallory's defenses. "You think I didn't know. I know everything like God. I knew about your trysts in college. That's why I sent for him. He'll leave you again. All I need to do is make the call."

The heart monitor beeps broke the silence between the two angry men. Mallory turned around and stared Malcolm down. He was no longer the injured man suffering from a heart ailment, but the ruthless man who would beat him severely on a daily basis when Mallory was little. "He'll never leave me. He'd die first. He promised me that."

"I can make that happen, too."

The heart monitor's alarm went off when Mallory towered over his bed. "You would do anything to break me, wouldn't you? Only a frightened man would go to great lengths to frighten his enemy." At that point, Mallory saw a twitch of fear in his father's face. He remembered that Uncle Murphy Lee said that he was afraid as well. The room grew dark and cold as a surge of power came over Mallory. His eyes grew icy blue and he began spewing out words that he didn't even understand. "Be careful, Dad. I'll succeed and you will bow to me. And if I'm not happy, you'll die by my hand." He straightened up and turned back to walk out.

"So, you have chosen. Matthew over the family."

"Matthew is family. He's my lover and no one will come between us, not even you, old man." He swung the door to find Marc standing out listening.

"You fucking faggot. You're a sick bitch." Marc pushed Mallory back in the room. Mallory deflected his brother's pushes. Marek floated in, noticing the tension. "We have a faggot in our midst." Marc pushed Mallory further in the room.

"Really?" Marek stepped aside trying to sound shocked.

"Marc, I don't have time for this rubbish." Mallory stomped toward him and commanded him to move. Marc snatched his arm and slung him on the hospital bed.

"What did you do, you fucking faggot? Why is Dad in this hospital bed?" Marc towered over him, shouting loudly.

Mallory got up and straightened his clothes. He looked over at Marek, but Marek avoided eye contact with him. Mallory decided playing the pitiful role wasn't working, so he thought being arrogant would.

"I fucked my bitch on Dad's desk."

Marek looked at him in horror.

"And I let him fuck me."

The whole room gasped. Marc balled up his fist and swung at Mallory, but Mallory caught his blow.

"I don't think so ... not today. Save your strength, you need to take care of this old man."

Marc retracted his fist and grabbed Mallory, throwing him up against the wall. Mallory's body slammed against the pale plastered wall. In the distance, he heard that familiar anger in Marc's voice. Malcolm somehow transferred his anger and fear into Marc. Before he knew it, Marc punched him several times in the abdomen. Powerless, Mallory slid to the floor.

"Get your ass up, bitch!"

Mallory could barely breathe. Sharp pains that he experienced in college when Matthew hit him grew across his chest. He struggled to his feet as he spit blood onto Marc's shirt.

"Is that it? You want more of Mallory? Would it make you feel better if I was lying next to Dad?" Mallory licked the blood off his lips.

"Yeah, it would." He went to punch Mallory again but he deflected the blows. He flung Marc on the bed and punched him several times in the face and chest. The heart monitor alarm went off again. Marek saw Malcolm grasping for breath. Marek pulled Mallory off and pushed him up against the wall.

"Stop! This is a fucking hospital. If we have to — let's take this outside."

"Fine. I'll meet you there." Mallory flung the door open and stormed out feverishly looking for the exit.

Marc attempted to follow him but Marek stopped him and patted Marc on the shoulder.

"Look I'll take care of him. You stay with Dad."

Mallory stormed out of the hospital. He sensed someone was behind him, so he quickly turned around and sucker punched whoever was behind him in the stomach. Marek went down but not before driving Mallory to the ground. They struggled, and Mallory managed to get on top. He pounded Marek in the face and chest. Marek kicked him off, and then quickly recovered to his feet to attack him.

"Shit, man, stop. I'm not the enemy." Marek said, wiping the blood from his mouth.

"You pissed at me, aye? I don't give a fuck who is pissed at me. If you want me, come get me."

"Well, what the fuck is wrong with you?"

"Marek, I'm sick of this shit. I'm bloody serious. I don't know what's going on. No one will tell and everyone is treating me like I'm some savior and some slimy piece of shit at the same time. I'm going to fucking explode." Mallory stomped back over to the double glass door and punched his fist through the glass, shattering it to pieces.

"Calm the fuck down." Marek said, resuming his battle stance.

"Why? You want me, aye?" Mallory stormed up to Marek, punching him again. Marek carefully deflected his punches but one connected and Marek fell to his knees.

"Not really. I admit I was pissed. But damn. Don't hit me no more, we don't need to fight."

Mallory stopped charging him and extended his hand out to Marek. Marek got up carefully holding his side.

"Marek, I'm serious. I don't have mental blocks! I'm not bullshitting people. I don't know what the fuck is going on!" He looked at Marek for sympathy, but he noticed that he was rubbing his side and not listening. "You know what? Fuck this. If you all want me, you bloody come get me. I'm not coming to you anymore." Mallory charged to his car. "And stay out of my got damn bedroom!" he shouted. He jumped in the car and slammed the door so hard that the driver side glass shattered into pieces. He started the car, backed up within inches of Marek' body then sped off. Marc walked out and found Marek limping through the bellowing exhaust.

"What the fuck? I said I was not going to take this ass whooping and I walked right in to it." He limped off. Marc rushed to his aid, grabbing his arm, and assisted Marek back into the hospital. He paused by the broken glass door and frowned. He examined Marek for cuts. "That could have been your head," Marek said, sulking.

CHAPTER FOUR

Mallory sped up to his gate, stopping short of the entrance. He spotted Harold working in the garage. He shot out of the car and rushed up to him. Harold looked up and saw Mallory marching toward him angrily. Mallory threw the keys in the air and shouted, "Get me another one!"

Harold caught the keys in mid-air, and then waited for Mallory go into the house. He strolled to the garage and picked up the phone. "Hello, this is Harold Rollins. Yes, it's that time again. It appears to be a broken window. Oh, the new 6-series came out yesterday. Well, I guess he's in luck. Can we have it delivered by tomorrow morning? Let's go with the white ... he tends to keep his white BMWs longer."

Mallory opened the back door looking for any presence of life in the house. He closed the door quietly and crept in slowly. He was so angry and confused, that seeing Matthew right now was not a good idea.

No one was around. He released a big sigh and walked toward the kitchen, grabbing a bottle of Vodka on the way. He opened the glass cabinet and pulled out a tall drinking glass. He opened the bottle and while preparing to pour it in the glass, he took a huge swig out of it.

As he turned the bottle up, he felt Matthew standing behind him. He turned around with the bottle still turned up and chugged the entire contents of the Vodka then threw the bottle in the sink, shattering it to pieces. They exchanged angry glares but neither one spoke. Matthew noticed Mallory's hand was bleeding, but before Matthew could say anything, Mallory stormed off to his master bathroom. He walked into the bathroom searching for a towel and antiseptic. Matthew leaned against the wall, allowing him to search around aimlessly. Mallory finally turned toward Matthew, who handed him the antiseptic. He snatched the bottle from Matthew's hand, and then looked around for a finger towel. Matthew handed him a clean finger towel. He snatched the towel as well. He turned the water on to rinse his hand.

"SSSSHHIITTT!" he screamed as he tried removing a piece of glass from his hand. Both hands began shaking as the blood gushed out. His body grew dizzy and he began collapsing. He mistakenly braced himself using his injured hand and when the pain shot through his arm, he fell to the floor. He cried out, but Matthew never moved or parted his lips. Mallory continued pulling out the glass piece, but it was too painful. Matthew just stood there.

Mallory finally looked up with a pathetic face. "Help me, please?"

Matthew slowly sat on the floor, grabbed his hand and carefully pulled out the pieces of glass. "Stay still," Matthew said calmly.

Mallory screamed and cursed as Matthew pulled several more pieces of glass out of his hand.

"Come on and get up now." He turned on the water and gently forced Mallory's hand under the stream, and then he gently poured the antiseptic over it. Mallory cringed, but Matthew held it tightly in place.

"SHIT!" He banged his other hand on the mirror.

"So you want the other hand to be hurt too?" Matthew said sarcastically. He carefully wrapped it tightly with a towel. "Please tell me the window looks worse than your hand."

"I guess."

"Did you go see Dad?"

"Uh-um, he's still alive."

"Did you talk to him?"

"Of course. I'm a pitiful faggot!" He shouted. "A waste. A little bitch that hides behind a bigger bitch." As Mallory yelled, Matthew rolled his eyes. "Marc was there. Everyone knows that little Mallory is a faggot now."

"That bothers you?"

"Not as much as you think." Mallory sat on the chaise lounge. "So when are you leaving me?"

"In two weeks." Matthew said, although he couldn't remember telling Mallory. "You're talking about the trip to Jerusalem, right?"

"So he's moving you to Egypt?"

"I'm not moving there. I'm meeting some friends from Oxford. Is that what we're talking about?"

"He said that you'd leave me. He's right. You know he's always right."

"Who, Dad? He doesn't know about the trip. I haven't told anyone."

"I know. Not even me."

"How did you know?"

"I didn't. Dad told me that you were leaving me and you confirmed it."

"Okay, I don't think we're talking about the same thing. I'm going on a business trip. You go on them all the time."

"He says you'll leave me and that he can make it happen."

"Emerald, I promised you that I would never leave you. Remember that? I said I would die first."

"Dying is so easy. You're still leaving."

"So what do you want me to do? Stay with you twenty-four hours a day? Would that make you feel better?"

Mallory glared at him. "Don't be cynical."

"What do you want me to say?"

"I just asked when you were going to leave me. It would be nice to know this time. I don't do well with surprises."

"Emerald, what else do you want me to say? I'm here for you. You don't believe me?"

"I believe you believe that for now. What happens in two weeks or one month?" Mallory jumped up from the chaise lounge, "When the thrill of the fuck is gone. What then?"

"You of all people should know that I'm not here for the fuck."

"You know, I'm beginning to realize that I don't know a got damn thing." Mallory walked toward the shower. When he slowly removed his shirt and undershirt, Matthew saw bruises on his body.

Once in the shower, Mallory braced himself against the wall allowing the water to massage his body. He opened a compartment and turned the dial to increase the water temperature. The steam bellowed up to the ceiling as burning drops of water pierced his body like needles. He pulled a lever down and the walls slammed down. Mallory was in solitude and his penance commenced. His screams echoed and bounced around the sealed cage as sharp lights flashed and blinded him. In his heighten rage; he banged his hands against the wall. The anger from his father and brothers surfaced and beat him to nothing. Mallory finally collapsed to the floor as blood poured from his body and ran down the drain.

Mallory crawled out of the shower and into the bedroom to find Matthew was asleep. He eased into bed, trying not to wake Matthew, but his eyes shot open as soon as he felt the sheets rustling. He allowed Mallory to settle in to bed before he rolled over and embraced him. He tried interlocking his fingers with Mallory's, but he tucked his hand underneath his body. Matthew sighed quietly, even though he wanted to scream. He retracted his embrace and rolled back over on his back.

"Emerald, I can't find the words to convince you that I'm going to stay. I know that you're angry, but I don't know who you're angry with. Yourself? Dad? I know with Dad but —" Matthew rambled nervously. "Is it me?" He waited for Mallory to respond, but there was only choking silence. He continued, "I don't know what Dad told you, but I'm not leaving you. If you're convinced that Dad is right, then take this opportunity and choose him...like I did all those years. Choose him. You deserve your family." He turned back over, grabbing his hand. "You deserve the best. Maybe I can't give you that. So, it's okay to choose him. I won't be angry with you...I promise. I'll understand." He paused, "But that would be it for me. I would dissolve. I can't exist without you." His tears fell on Mallory's face. "I can't breathe without you. But I'll understand. I need you. Emerald, please talk to me. Please?"

"Matthew, I think I need to throw up." Mallory said coldly.

Mallory crawled out of bed and returned to the bathroom, slamming the door behind him. He sat on the floor next to the toilet and leaned over the cold bowl. Falling tears fell from his eyes and into the bowl, causing distorted ripples. The voices of failure, pleadings and anger were shouting in his head. As the pain from his hand grew, Mallory's body shut down and he soon passed out.

He woke up hours later to find himself covered with a thermal blanket and his hand dressed with clean gauzes. He looked down and saw a ring on his finger. It was Matthew's special ring and he never let it out of his sight. Matthew loved this ring. His mother gave him that ring and he always boasted that it was "blessed" and vowed to never part with it. Mallory took the ring off and read an inscription; *"To second chances,"* He got up and strolled out of the bathroom, looking for Matthew, but he wasn't in bed. He looked down and noticed Matthew asleep by the door.

If he leaves, I'll survive. But would he? Mallory stooped down and grabbed Matthew's hand, waking him. "Come here." He led Matthew to the family room and sat him down on the chaise lounge. He put his favorite French movie in the player and sat down next to him.

"Emerald, what are you doing?"

"Lie down with me ..."

Matthew found a comfortable spot and Mallory snuggled next to him.

"I guess ... what I want is for you to hold me like you did the first time we — or shall I say you — watched this movie."

"Can I tell you the truth?" Matthew asked, playing with Mallory's long lashes. "I wasn't watching this movie. It was just on when you snuggled next to me. I hated this movie. I just didn't wanna get up to change the channel because you felt so good. I wanted to watch sports."

"Here's the remote, ass."

"I love this movie now. It reminds me of you, of us at that time. How carefree we were."

"I miss us. I want us - the way we were in college. Before Malcolm and all the Haulms." He squeezed him tightly. "Baby, I don't wanna fight about who's leaving whom. I feel like this would be a never-ending argument that would throw us in circles. I don't wanna be in circles."

"No circles. Just a great ride." He bit his ear.

"Keep the movie on and let it watch us." Mallory pulled Matthew close, planting full and wet kisses on his body.

Marek stood in the doorway of Mallory's office. He wanted to charge in, but he remembered the last time he rushed into of one of Mallory's rooms. He didn't want to relive that chaotic horror. Standing outside his door, he observed Mallory in his element. He thought he recognized the person behind the desk, but was that the same Mallory he had reunited with two years ago? He didn't look the same. Maybe Marek was seeing Mallory for the first time, the baby who overcame all those years of abuse.

Marek stood there and wondered, did he ever heal from the pain or was he suppressing it by acting out for attention. Indeed this mystery that Marek was eager to crack, but he didn't want to do anything would have him lose Mallory again. He gently knocked on the door, but Mallory didn't respond.

Melody walked up and noticed Marek standing in the doorway. "Hi sweetie."

"Hello ma'am. I just came by to see Mallory."

"Go on in. You don't need a formal announcement," she said pushing him through the door. "MALLORY!" She shouted. "See! Just yell at him. He'll respond."

Mallory looked up and pulled out earplugs. "True, but how is the question," He huffed. "How long you have been standing there?"

"Just for a minute. I knocked." Marek said defensively.

"I was listening to music. It helps me concentrate."

"Hmm. What are you listening to?"

"Bach."

"Who?"

Mallory snickered. "What do you need?"

"I wanted to see if you were okay. You know we... well I haven't heard from you in a month."

"I figured – you heard what I said that day. I wasn't coming to you and I meant it."

"Oh, I see. So you can just cut us out like that. Is it that easy for you?"

"Easy? You think it's easy? Think about it. I don't remember spending that much time with you guys when I was little. I was always in the hospital or somewhere else. I got snatched away from the only family I knew for what, fourteen years, to live where? I don't even remember."

"You were with Uncle Mal."

"That's what everybody tells me. I don't remember that. Then everybody gets angry with me because I don't remember things. Easy, you say?" He shook head. "When I returned and saw you guys again, I finally felt part of something. I thought I had a family again. All to get snatched away again. Easy, you say?"

"Alright, maybe easy is not the correct word." He wanted to change the subject. "I guess you fag— I mean homo-sex-u-als can fight, uh?"

Mallory huffed. "Yes we can. Unbelievably, compared to Matthew, I fight like a little girl. His temper is cooler than mine. He can whoop somebody's ass and never lose his cool."

"Is he okay? Are you two okay?"

"We'll get through it. I still have this fear in my heart that Malcolm was right about him leaving me, but I can't harp on that. All I can do is enjoy him now." Mallory said, trying to convince himself that he was not worried.

Marek started fidgeting.

"What is it Marek?"

"Look, I ain't Keith Sweat, so I ain't going to be begging you and shit, but we need you. You said if we needed you, to come and get you. Not to ask or beg."

"I see that I'm going to have to be literal with you."

"Yep. Anyway, we need you. We're a family. We need to get this on."

"So what am I supposed to do?"

"For starters, you need to start attending the Black Knighthood meetings."

"What in the bloody hell is a Black Knighthood meeting?" Mallory asked. He saw Marek getting frustrated. "Marek, I don't know! Just tell me."

"Just show up at the Embassy Towers tomorrow night at nine. If it doesn't jog your memory, I'll answer all of your questions."

"Do I need to wear black?"

"Hell nawh," He laughed. "With them heavy ass black robes we have to wear, you might wanna be naked." They laughed, and then Marek remembered whom he was talking to. "Wait, don't do that shit!" Marek started to walk out and Mallory called out to him.

"Hey Marek... do you think ... we can ... hmm ...hang out sometime?"

"Shit yeah. You still have some female freak in you cuz I ain't going to no gay club!"

"I'll let you drag me to a strip club. Just don't tell Matthew."

CHAPTER FIVE

Matthew was gone on his second trip to Jerusalem. He and Mallory kept in contact by phone and email, but they missed the physical connection. That night, Mallory was working late in the office preparing for an SEC audit. The SEC changed some rules and regulations and Mallory's company was always used for target practice.

In prior years, Mallory didn't mind the attention. This was a free outside audit service for him. He was always assured that he wasn't going to be punished for any violations of any rules that were not yet published. This also gave him the opportunity to break in any new beautiful female agents.

However, this year was different. The entire exercise was cumbersome. He endured long nights defending his actions and finding further clarifications for his decisions. Furthermore, Mallory was not going to be able to enjoy his *"Pass the Audit"* party that he threw every year for the female agents.

Mallory was painfully reviewing files and preparing for the auditors. Natasha, one of the interns, volunteered to help him since Melody was out on vacation.

"Natasha?" he screamed. "Copy this for me?" He rubbed his eyes, patiently waiting for Matthew to get online.

"Here you go," She handed him the copies and picked up more files to copy. "No word?"

"No word on what?"

"I know you're waiting for Matthew."

"Am I that obvious?"

"YES. He gets online between nine and ten. I know you wanted to be home but you got that call from Marek, so you're stuck here waiting."

"I AM that obvious. You think I'm sprung?"

"Uh... yeah." She rolled her eyes.

"Get out of here and pull those reports for me."

"Fine." She walked out of the room. Moments later, Mallory heard her scream.

"Are you okay?"

"I'm fine. I just scared myself," she said. Mallory laughed at her expense. As he worked on his spreadsheet, his Windows Messenger flashed.

"Hey Emerald, I heard this song and thought of you." The message flashed and a file appeared named Captain and Tennille.

Mallory clicked on the file and the song started.

"Do that to me one more time, once is never enough, with a man like you. Do that to me one more time; I can never get enough of a man like you... ohh."

Mallory banged his head on his desk several times when Natasha walked in his office.

"What is wrong with you?"

"EVERYTHING!" he cried. "He keeps sending me these songs and they keep making me horny. I miss him so much. I can't take it anymore."

"Damn, you got it bad."

"I don't need comments from you, Usher," Mallory shouted.

She laughed and walked out of his office.

Mallory typed. "You can't make requests like this over the net."

"Why not?" He typed.

"You have to ask? I'm better in person. You need to stop this shit. I have a woman in my office and I'm not afraid to use her."

Natasha laughed and Mallory looked up again. "What are you doing?" he screamed.

"Nothing!" She shouted. "Are you ready to go?"

"No, I'm still working." Mallory returned to the message.

The message flashed. "Do you want me?"

"YES."

"What would you do?"

"At this point... anything?"

"Really?"

Natasha walked back into the office. "We can't get any more ready for the audit. I'm going to shut down, is that okay?"

"Yes. Yes. I'm right behind you." He never looked up. She sat on the couch but Mallory lost sense that she was there. He continued tennis-typing communication with Matthew.

"Sing to me." The message flashed.

"Sing to you? This is IM, not web cam."

"I can hear you if you sing."

"No you can't."

"Yes, I can. I love your voice. I'll hear it in my mind. Do it. I promise it will make you feel better."

He huffed. "Bloody hell... fine. It better make me feel better." He started singing. "Oh baby... do that to me once again."

The message flashed. "Louder."

"Oh baby... do that to me once again." He elevated his voice a bit.

"Louder!"

Mallory closed his eyes and bellowed out. "Oh oh oh oh oh baby ..." The session went offline. "... Do that to me one more time."

Seconds later a bass voice sung. "Do it again."

Mallory's eyes followed the voice to find Matthew standing in the doorway.

"Hey Emerald."

Mallory was so excited he couldn't move from his chair. Matthew walked toward him, leaned over his desk and kissed him.

"Okay, that's too much." Natasha sprung up.

Mallory broke the kiss, frowning. "Are you still here?"

"Yeah! He said he could get you to sing and I wanted to see it."

"Bitch!"

"Are you calling me a —"

"No, Natasha, not you!" He finally got up and turned off his computer.

"And what do you mean that you're not afraid to use me?" Natasha continued her rant.

"You set me up." Mallory pulled Matthew up against him and nuzzled his face in his chest. "I missed you."

"Hold it until we get home. I wanna hear all about it." Matthew wrapped his arms around him and squeezed him tightly.

𝔐

Once they reached the garage, Mallory opened the car door for Matthew. He jumped in and opened the door from the inside for Mallory. Once inside, Mallory grabbed his face and planted a long awaited kiss. Being temporarily satisfied, he sped off.

"So how was your Klan meeting?" Matthew said jokingly. "What's it really called again?"

"Black Knighthood meeting. It's freaky weird. You have to wear these heavy black robes and the meeting is held in this dark room lighted only by candles. They say these bizarre chants. I was going to look them up tonight. They seemed like they were talking in opposites."

"What do you mean?"

"Well this one guy got up and announced that famine was down due to the rise in donations from the global humanity."

"That's good, aye?"

"I thought so, but they were pissed. This other guy was discussing the peace talk breakouts like they were the start of a plague."

"Plague?"

"Oh, oh! They were livid about the death toll. They said people were living longer and healthier lives and that it had to be stopped."

"Shit?"

"The fucked up thing about it is then they turned to me and asked me what I was going to do about it. It was my department."

"What happened?"

"I froze. Malcolm stood up and said not to worry because we're taking care of it. The Proselytization will take place by the next solar eclipse."

"Who – seli– zation?"

"Proselytization. I don't know what it is and they won't tell me about it. All I know is it some kind of conversion. It sounds painful, probably have to eat a live chicken, kiss a snake or some shit."

Matthew laughed. "You already eat chicken; maybe it will be a live cow."

"Gross. You know I hate beef."

"When is the next solar eclipse?"

"I don't know. I was trying to look it up. There are several of them. I think it's the one in June. That's the one that will be seen in the northern hemisphere."

"All of this for an executive position at the company?"

"I don't think so. It was all the same people but I don't think this has anything to do with the company." He paused. "They haven't told me what I'm supposed to be doing there or what department I'm heading up."

"That's weird. We already have a CFO."

"I wish you were still there." Mallory grabbed his hand. "You could snoop and give me some news."

"I haven't given my notice yet, I'm just on leave. I'll check it out and let you know."

"Thanks." He grabbed his hand. "Hey ... how was your dig?"

"Man you wouldn't believe it. We found the first samurai sword that was created for the first angel of death."

"No shit?"

"Yeah, it's said that it will find its way back to the final angel of death."

"What are you researching?"

"Revelations." He mumbled.

"Revelations, I heard that. Why?"

"I have this purpose or yearning to find answers." Matthew said vaguely, not wanting to get into an in-depth conversation about religion and God. "I started something in college and I'm just finishing it."

"To what? Are you trying to see if God exists?"

"He does exist."

"Of course he does, to the blind, weak and destitute," Mallory said sarcastically.

"Which one are you?" Matthew snapped sharply.

"None of them. I don't believe in that rubbish." Mallory hated discussing religion or God. That discussion was sure to cause bitter feelings and guaranteed to kill the mood.

"Emerald, you have to believe in something."

"I do?" Mallory rolled his eyes. "Well then, I believe in myself. I do good and I do evil but I don't let that define me. I don't need a higher power to tell me that I'm good or evil." As Mallory continued his tirade, Matthew donned his guilt complex armor. "And what defines good and evil? It's just little compartments for people to place themselves in when they are too scared to face the truth."

"What's the truth?"

"We're alone. There is no higher power. There is no greater good out there that saves people from disease or pain, or even death. Some nut, such as King James, wanted ultimate control over his subjects, so he created this God to instill fear in their hearts. And if there were any type of God, he's a weak one. I mean, evil exists, what can stop it? If he were all powerful, there would be no evil."

"No evil? Do you not think that evil exists because of free will? Man was given free will." Matthew's voice changed, but Mallory was too caught up in his tirade to see the trap.

"Fuck free will. What about it? You can't have it both ways. You can't tell a person that they have free will then guilt them to control them. That's chaotic."

"You're so asinine. God is everywhere. In the air you breathe, the bottled water you obsessively drink, the ability to think such insane thoughts. That's God. God exists merely in the miracles we see today.

"Miracles?" Mallory grunted.

"Oh my God, you don't believe in miracles?"

"I do. Miracles are extraordinary events that happen, but a person's educational background or experience can't explain it. It doesn't mean that it's not explainable. They don't possess the knowledge to explain it or understand it. I perform financial miracles everyday. So am I God?"

"Emerald, you're a true atheist."

"And you're confused." Mallory shouted. "Everything that has happened can be scientifically or mathematically explained." Mallory continued to raise his voice to prove his point.

Matthew released a long sigh then became silent.

Mallory finally realized that Matthew set a trap, and he fell in. He quickly grabbed his hand and said softly, "Is it that important to you for me to believe in God?"

"Kinda." He mumbled and rolled eyes.

"Kinda? That's not good enough. This is a big step here."

"Then yeah, it's important. It's damn important," Matthew said angrily.

"Okay ..." He leaned over, grabbing Matthew's face and kissing him, "Will you be my God?" Mallory said jokingly but was very serious about his question.

"You're so full of bullshit. I don't know why I even bother. This is serious to me."

"I am serious. I believe in you. You're strong and powerful. You can protect me and control me." He flashed a witty smile and glazed his hand on the side of Matthew's cheek. "I already worship the ground you walk on. And I sing praises to you every time you make me …"

"Stop Emerald!" Matthew smirked, grabbing his hand and kissing it.

"I'm really serious, baby. Will you be my God?" Mallory looked in his eyes.

"Yeah, I'll be your God." He smirked and joked, "And I guess you wanna be mine."

Mallory peeked at him from the corner of his eyes. "Are you sure about that?" He said sharply. "You know, I'm a very jealous God and I have no tolerance for those who worship other Gods before me."

"You're an ass." Matthew threw Mallory hand's back. "I can't believe you Emerald. You can be such a self-centered, shallow prick of a demonic—"

"I was kidding…stop."

"No, that's the point. You're not kidding. You're so self-diluted in your own world that it becomes toxic. How do you breathe? The shit that you talk is so contaminated with your delusions that it's sickening."

"Matty, please stop. Let's stop talking about this, aye?" Mallory felt the guilt swelling from inside. "Look, I'll believe in God if you want."

"IT'S NOT ABOUT FUCKING GOD! IT'S ABOUT YOU!" Matthew shouted in a sinister tone. "You're selfish! Anything that is greater than what your over-developed pea brain can handle, you dismiss it like it doesn't exist."

"Why are you saying this to me?" Mallory's voice wavered as his heart shattered to pieces.

"You're so close to being perfect, but you anger me with your small mindedness." Matthew finally looked over and saw Mallory broken. He turned his head toward the window and smiled. He loved having Mallory in a vulnerable position.

Matthew's words shattered Mallory and left him heartbroken. As he stared blankly out of the window, the words soaked in deeper than Matthew anticipated.

Mallory realized that the conversations with Matthew were becoming more abusive and controlling, to the point that he began second-guessing his thoughts and actions. Mallory was accustomed to living his life according to the guidelines he created, and life was good for him. But each day with Matthew, Mallory's good life suffered horrendous beatings.

As his mind drifted in thought, so did his eyes. He didn't notice the bright headlights in his lane bearing down toward him. Matthew finally looked forward and saw the car speeding toward them at a fast pace so he yelled out. Mallory quickly jerked the wheel, barely missing the other car, and sent the Jaguar in to 360-degree spinout. The car finally slammed against the concrete median. They both gasped when they witnessed the other car break through the steel barricade and flew off the road down into a ravine.

"Shit!" Matthew breathed. "What should we do?"

"Call the ambulance," Mallory said as he tossed the cell phone to Matthew and jumped out of the car.

"What are you doing?"

"I'm going to see if he is alright!"

"How do you know that it's a he? He or she could be dead."

"I don't feel that he's dead. I can't explain it, but he's not dead." Mallory rushed to the other side of car. "Do what I said and call the ambulance!"

"Emerald, stop! Let's think this through. You can get hurt down there. Look, let's call some people and wait up here. Emerald, why are you sacrificing yourself?"

"First you ream me for being selfish! Now you're chewing my ass for wanting to save someone? Don't think I didn't get the fact that you blew our conversation out of sort because you want to be on top! I'll deal with that later. But for now, I have to save him. Call the bloody ambulance!" Mallory ran across the highway and down the ravine into the dark.

Matthew sat back in the car and threw the cell phone in the backseat.

CHAPTER SIX

It was Matthew's fifth or sixth trip to Jerusalem, Mallory couldn't remember. All Mallory knew was that he was gone for three months this time and he missed Matthew terribly. He started feeling cold and empty. He knew there were many temporary fixes for his dilemma, but only two possible long-lasting solutions: Matthew or Brielle. He couldn't be with Matthew tonight because it would take his crew two hours to file a flight plan and another several hours to travel. He couldn't be with Brielle because he promised Matthew that he was going to be faithful.

Brielle started calling him at the most 'needed times'. This made Matthew worry. So far, Mallory was doing well. But tonight, Mallory's mind began screaming and his body aching. As he drove home, he received a call from Brielle.

"Damn!" He shouted. Not able to resist, he answered the call. "Towneson."

"Hello, my almighty." Brielle's lustful voice answered.

"How are you doing?"

"Not well ... I miss you."

"Is that right?"

"Where are you?"

"I'm fifteen minutes from home."

"I want you tonight."

"You wanna see me tonight?"

"No, Mallory. I want you tonight. You crave me and I feel it."

Mallory didn't respond.

"I thought we made a beautiful connection."

"We did. I just ..."

"Made a commitment to Matthew. I know you told me. But he can never satisfy you like I have."

"Brielle, he satisfies me very well."

"Really? Why do I hear coldness and emptiness in your voice?"

"He's not here and I just miss him."

"I would never leave you alone."

"I know. He said that same thing ... but he's a professional just as I am. It's part of the game. Sometimes you have to be away and I understand that."

"Mallory, a man in your position should never have to understand. You should just have."

Mallory smiled as her words seeped through his boundary.

"My love, don't you ache for my warmth and sensual touch?"

"You need to stop."

"Why don't you drop by tonight?"

"I don't do booty calls, Brielle."

"Well then bring a suit. I'll cook breakfast. I believe you like my waffles better."

"You're really tempting me."

"Bring my yellow condom ... bring your little black one too. Believe me, I'll feel much better than your Matthew."

Mallory sucked in air through his teeth.

"Close your eyes, Mallory, and imagine my hair falling on your body and my hands caressing your chest. Can you taste my breasts in your mouth ... can you feel my moisture?"

"Brielle, I'm driving! You really need to stop."

"I won't stop until I feel you inside me."

"Well hold on and let me pull over." He managed to pull over to the curb and placed the call on mute. He banged his head on the steering wheel several times. *Damn you Matthew! You're testing my patience here. What to do, what to do, what to do?* He took a deep breath and took the phone off mute. "Brielle ..."

"Yes?"

"You're so tempting. I ..." He tried to find the words to say no. "... will be over tonight." Just as he finished his statement, call waiting beeped in. "Hey can you hold on for a minute?"

"Don't make me wait long."

Mallory switched to the other line, "Towneson."

"Hey Emerald."

"Oh shit! I'm so happy to hear from you. Where are you? Damn that ... I'll have them rush the flight plan and I can be there in less than ten hours."

"Emerald, calm down."

"Damn calm ... I need you! I want you so bad. Matty, I'm DYING!"

"Emerald, where are you?"

"I'm at the bend, ten minutes from home."

"Well hurry. I have a surprise for you."

Mallory grinned, "Really?"

"Yeah, when you get home turn on your web cam."

"My web cam? Matty, Internet sex? Oh hell no! I can't do Internet sex tonight."

"Calm down, Emerald."

"What am I supposed to do, cum all over the screen again?"

Matthew laughed. "I wouldn't do that unless you wanna buy another monitor again. You're so wild. No, I have a surprise for you."

"This is rubbish Matty ... I have been waiting ..."

"Three months, fourteen days, 15 hours ... nine minutes, and counting. You're wasting time." He completed his statement.

"Fine. Internet sex ... this is a new low for me."

"Emerald, I'm hurt."

"Sorry, I was supposed to say that silently."

"Come home, baby. I promise you will enjoy it." There was strange silence. "What's wrong?"

"Nothing. I'll be there."

Matthew knew the tone in his voice that he was wavering. "Emerald, I love you."

"I love you, too."

"Then what's wrong?"

"Nothing, I'm on my way home."

Matthew heard his voice crack that time. "Who called?"

Mallory paused. He remembered that Brielle was on the other line and that was taboo. He promised Matthew that he wouldn't have any contact with her. He couldn't lie to him. He never lied before. He thought hard, "Angela?"

"Angela?" He grunted. "Look, I'll make a deal with you. Come home and get on the web cam. If you're still not satisfied, you can go see ..." he paused, "Angela."

"I'm on my way." Mallory hung up the phone and it beeped again. "Damn, I'm sorry. Something has come up and I can't come right now."

"I understand," Brielle said softly.

"Thank you for your understanding. Hey, don't wait up for me, but don't be mad if I wake you tonight, okay?"

"Hopefully, I'll see you later. Good night."

Mallory hung up the phone and drove off. When he finally made it home, he noticed the valet, Harold, waiting for him at the end of the driveway.

"Evening?" Mallory said inquisitively, getting out of the car.

"Evenin'. Peter had to leave on an urgent matter. But I'll take good care of yah." Harold grabbed the keys from Mallory's hands.

"Thanks. Is everything okay with Peter?"

"Yeah, he said he'd be back in a couple of days."

"Thank you, good night." Mallory walked up to the house looking for his house key. *Matthew and Peter are both gone. I'm fucked.* He opened the door to a dark house. He looked around to find every light off, except something flickering in the distance. He looked back to see Harold watching him. He waved and then disappeared into the dark garage.

Mallory closed the door and walked toward the flickering light. It was a large candle. He looked down the hall and spotted another candle. He followed the candles upstairs where the last candle was at the door to his office. He opened the door to find that it was dark as well. The only light in the room was his monitor. As he walked toward the monitor, a message was flashing.

"Emerald Open Me!"

He sat at his desk and clicked on the screen.

"Your web cam is broken."

"BULLSHIT! THIS IS BLOODY FUCKING BULLSHIT," he screamed.

"Emerald. You can fix it," the message flashed.

"How the bloody hell am I going to fix it?" He screamed at the computer, but it didn't respond. "This is rubbish." Mallory picked up the phone and started to call Brielle when another message popped on the screen.

"Emerald I'm worth it."

"I know. I'm sorry." He put the phone down. "How can I fix it?" He typed.

"Go to the satellite and tilt it back into position."

"WHAT! I don't know where my bloody satellite is," he shouted at the computer again, and then typed: "Horny man doesn't know where satellite is!"

"It's on the roof right outside your office."

"Now I'm supposed to kill my damn self?"

"I'm worth it."

Mallory closed his eyes. "Yes, you are." He took off his suit coat, removed his cufflinks and rolled up his sleeves. He opened the sliding window to his office and climbed out on the terrace. It was a cloudless night with a light wind and a beautifully bright full moon. "This better be good." He found the stairs that would take him to the roof. As he took his first step, he looked down then stood frozen, clamping himself to the stairs.

"This is a real new low. I need to look into that celibacy thing."

He took a deep breath and started his ascent to the roof. His head barely reached the top of the stairs when he saw another flickering light. Once, he reached the top, he found Matthew on the roof sitting at a well-dressed dinner table with his laptop.

Matthew transformed the rooftop into a lover's nest, complete with a down comforter with fluffy pillows and many hurricane candles. Mallory beamed with every step he took toward Matthew who was dressed in all white and his lustful smile completed his ensemble when he flashed his pearly white teeth.

"Tell me that you're a hologram." Mallory said as he held him tight.

"No. I'm just your angel." Matthew took a deep breath and squeezed him back.

"I missed you so," Mallory said. Matthew went to kiss him but he stopped him by placing his hands on Matthew's chest. "It was Brielle who called," he confessed.

"I know. I'm just happy that you decided to come home."

"Matty, I can't stand this distance. I know I said that I could ... but I can't."

Matthew held his face and slipped a kiss on his lips. "Let's not talk about that right now. Are you hungry?"

Mallory caught a whiff of irresistible aroma. "Starving."

"Well sit here and I'll serve you tonight."

Mallory saw strawberries and a glass filled with his favorite white wine. "Strawberries," he said, biting into the sweet fruit. "Umm, soaked in Grand Marnier. My three favorites: you, lobster and strawberries." He ate the rest of the strawberry while watching Matthew.

Matthew frowned a bit. "I hope in that order." Matthew served Mallory lemon grilled lobster with basil mashed potatoes and a vegetable medley. He prepared his plate and they enjoyed their delicious dinner by candle and moonlight.

Just as they finished their meal, Matthew got up, grabbed the platter of strawberries along with Mallory's hand, and led him to a fluffy pallet he prepared.

"This is nice," Mallory said. Matthew sat down and Mallory laid his head on his leg. He took a strawberry and traced the outline of Mallory's lips. "This is wonderful." Mallory bit into the strawberry.

"I told you that I was worth it. You're worth it too. Don't think that you were the only one suffering."

"Really, sometimes you make me feel like I'm some sex-crazed animal."

"You are!" He laughed. "You're a borderline nymphomaniac. I love you for that. I crave you too, but I'm just more subtle."

Mallory sat up and kissed Matthew. "Subtle uh? So you did miss me?"

Matthew laid back and Mallory crawled along side of him. "You know I did. I dreamed this whole thing the second that I got on the plane." He unbuttoned Mallory's shirt and slipped his hands inside it to remove it from his pants. "Do you think your neighbors have telescopes?"

"If they do, they will learn a new type of astronomy tonight."

Early the next morning, Matthew woke up to find Mallory sitting at the table. "What are you doing?"

"I didn't want to wake you, but there are school children in our neighborhood. I don't want to be the reason for their sex education this morning."

"How responsible of you."

"Somebody has to be ..."

"You?"

"I'm trying. Anyway, I cleaned the roof and I'm going in to take a shower. Make me breakfast?"

"I'm your bitch now?"

"I thought we would switch off that role and this month you can play the bitch. Please?" Mallory pouted.

"Alright. Waffles?"

"Yeah, you know I like yours best."

"I bet you say that to Brielle too. You're not going to work, are you?"

"M-huh."

"I thought maybe we could spend the day together."

"Baby, I'll be home tonight. I'll even leave early."

Matthew paused. "I'm leaving tomorrow morning."

"What? This is bloody rubbish!" he screamed.

"Look, I came back for you, but I'm not finished."

Mallory grabbed an empty wine bottle and threw it off the roof. "This is bloody rubbish, Matthew! Oh is it a good time now to talk about the distance?"

"Yeah it is," Matthew bowed his head.

"I don't like it. You're gone two or three months at a time. I can't take this."

"I know, but I'm so close to finding answers."

"Answers to what? You won't even tell me what you're looking for."

"Emerald, you don't care."

"How in the hell can I care if I don't know? It's that God shit, isn't it?" Matthew shook his head. "Fucking fine! Why don't you fuck God next time?" Mallory stormed off the roof. Matthew laid back down and pulled the comforter over his head.

Mallory walked into the kitchen to find Harold glancing at the stove. "What's wrong?" he barked.

"Well I heard you and Matthew arguing so I figured I would have to cook breakfast," Harold said looking puzzled at the stove.

He laughed. "Harold, Peter doesn't cook."

Harold heaved a sigh of relief, but Mallory continued.

"But he does hand me my towel when I get out of the shower."

Horror struck his face and Mallory laughed.

"I can get my own towel and believe it or not, I can even dress myself. You just get my car ready, okay?"

"Thanks, Mallory." He patted Harold on the back and walked out of the kitchen into his bedroom. He grabbed his beeping cell phone that was on the bed. He pushed the speakerphone to retrieve the message. It was from Brielle. He stopped the message, closed the door then continued it.

"Hello my almighty. I missed you last night. I hope he satisfied you. You do realize he will never fully satisfy your deepest desires, don't you? Tell Matthew that he won this fight, but the battle is far from over."

"Battle? Women," he said shaking his head then threw the phone back on the bed and walked into the master bathroom. On his way, he hit the shower button as he headed toward the toilet. "Men! They're no better!"

Matthew finally made it off the roof and walked into the kitchen. Harold was standing at the espresso machine with a look of confusion painted on his face. "Trying to make coffee ... I don't know how to work the damn thing."

"Don't worry," Matthew said. "You want coffee?"

"Yeah, I also wanna make some for Mallory."

"Never serve Emerald coffee, trust me, you'll regret it." Matthew went to the espresso machine and turned it on. "Just like I regret a lot of things," He said under his voice.

"You call him Emerald?"

"It's the eyes. I'm a damn sucker for those eyes. That's probably how I get in these fucking situations, those gorgeous green eyes."

"So when are you making the waffles?" Harold asked.

"I haven't decided if I'm making them."

"You will."

"I will what? Decide or make them."

"Make them," Harold smiled. "Peter told me about you two."

"Really, what did he say?" Matthew grabbed two cups and handed Harold a cup.

"That you two are opposite sides of a coin. You two always give in to each other. Mallory appears to be happy. I know. He has kept the same car almost a year and he doesn't normally do that. He either changes them out or destroys them. Usually destroys them."

"Destroys them?" He sat at the bar next to Harold.

"Oh yeah, he would get so angry that he would race home and would lose control at that bend. He wrapped at least eight cars around that old oak tree."

"Damn. Was he hurt?"

"Nawh, he walked away from every one of them crashes with nothing that a Band-Aid and some Campho-Phenique couldn't cure. They wanted to put him in a psych ward one time. They tried to label him suicidal. He even had to go to a shrink."

"What happened?"

"I think he had sex with the doctor and she released him," he chuckled, shaking his head.

"Damn, learn something new. Tell me more."

Harold held his hands up. "Look, I like working for him and this gig is the best I ever had so I don't wanna make waves."

"You're not making waves, don't worry. Tell me more." Matthew walked into the pantry and grabbed the items for the waffles not realizing what he was doing.

"Mallory has an evil temper."

"I know he gets angry but... evil? That's a little harsh."

"Peter told me that, one time, he was so angry at this man that his eyes filled with ice and the man fell dead at his feet."

"Peter said that?"

"Yeah, he said Mallory was so cold to the touch that he spent hours in that shower. You know he has a special hot water heater for that shower." Harold took a big sip of his hot coffee wondering if he should continue. "He's worried about you, you know?"

"Who Peter?"

"Yeah! He said you shouldn't be here, but I think that Mallory's happy. Are you happy?"

"Yes, I am. Why would Peter say that I'm not supposed to be here?"

"He said something about you being blinded and missing your purpose. That if you stay, it will only end in disaster. That's why Peter left, to be sure that you are who he thinks you are."

Matthew scratched his head. "Who does he think that I am?"

"The son of God."

"Who?"

"Yeah, not only the son of God but the—"

Mallory walked out of the bedroom into the kitchen startling both Matthew and Harold. "I'm sorry. I just miss you so much," Mallory held him closely. "I hate this distance, baby."

"It's not you. I'll delay my trip, okay? I still wanna spend the day with you."

"You do? Let's go to the Gallery."

"Not Brielle's Gallery."

"Matty! Why would we go there?" He pinched his cheeks. "Why don't you take a shower and we'll head down to Houston. They have a new religious exhibit showing I know you'll love, and we can go to The Galleria. You know you like that one better than Dallas. Don't worry. I'll make the waffles."

"How bitch of you."

"I'll take the bitch role today." Mallory smiled at the bowl of batter. "Perfect! He already mixed it!"

Mallory packed some things in the Range Rover while Matthew programmed the stereo and loaded the CDs. They settled in the truck and drove away. As they drove past the bend, Mallory slowed down a little. Matthew wanted to ask him about his accidents but he promised Harold that he wouldn't involve him in any discussions.

"Damn that tree looks bad."

"Yeah, it's in a bad spot. I had a couple of minor accidents there."

"Just a couple?" He softly prodded.

"Yeah, just a couple. Well more than a couple... well more like eight or nine."

"Damn and you're still walking?"

"Yes, I suffered a scratch or something. I think the last time I re-cracked my rib. Nothing major."

"They still let you drive?"

"For a moment there, they took my license and made me go to anger management sessions. One time they thought that I was trying to commit suicide. That was a joke."

"Were you?"

"No! I was just angry."

"At what?"

"Anything. Back then, anything would set me off. But I'm fine now."

"Did you go see somebody about it?"

"They made me, but I fucked her. She was so easy," he said smiling. "Beautiful too." Mallory looked over at Matthew's puzzled face. "What's up?"

"Nothing. So you were healed?"

"Healed? You use the strangest words. No, I just got over it. It really helped when I got that shower. It calms me down and soothes me."

"On the setting that beats the shit out of your body."

"It's intense, I'll admit, but it helps me. I can scream or cry or anything. When I get out, I feel a release. A catharsis."

"You scream? I have never heard you scream in the shower."

"It's sound proof."

"What?"

"It's sound proof, has temperature control and is virtually indestructible. I can turn the water on as hot as I need it. I can hit the walls or anything. At the end of the shower, it all goes down the drain."

"That's why you don't like me in the shower with you."

"Yes, that's why."

"You're a tortured soul."

"You wouldn't have me any other way," Mallory wanted to play 100 questions with him but he didn't know how to approach the situation.

"Okay ... I guess it's my turn. Ask away."

"I know I'm jaded and I have warped values. I want to know what you're doing. I mean, what's so important that it made you quit the company and keeps you away from me."

"Emerald, I didn't quit, I took a leave of absence and you don't wanna know."

"I do want to know. Look, I'll keep an open mind, and I'll keep any sarcastic commentaries to myself. I want to know. You're important to me, and I think it's important to know."

"Seriously?"

"Yes."

"Okay, it's a continuation of the research I started when I was in college."

"For a class?"

"No, it wasn't for a class... it's more like a calling." Matthew started.

Mallory tried to hide the frown that crept across his face.

"Do you wanna hear this or not?"

"Just tell me."

"Okay," he continued. "There are people who believe they can identify the fourth horseman. Do you know the story of the four horsemen?"

"Of the apocalypse? As in the book of Revelations."

"You do know the Bible?"

"Yes, extremely well. It's a very important historical document written by some very important people."

"It's a living word that God wrote." Matthew defended sharply.

Mallory bit his tongue and allowed Matthew to continue.

"Well we believe —"

"We?"

"I believe it." He looked over at Mallory's grimacing face. "We believe that there are clues to help us identify him. There have been signs that tell us how to find him. We had the family line narrowed down. It seems that these charges cross to different races and are passed down through the male generation – brothers, cousins and uncles."

"So what's so important about this fourth one? Aren't the other three important?"

"Yeah, they're serious but the fourth one is death. It ends with him."

"Oh, well I guess if I were going to be one, I would want to be the fourth one ... such a cocky position. It fits me."

Matthew chuckled. "Yes it does baby, fits you perfectly! Like I was saying, the other three are serious. But their methods take a long time and are often combated with love and compassion from humanity. But the fourth one is like a thief in the night."

"Oh," Mallory smiled. "A sneaky motherfucker. I like him already."

"I bet you do!"

"So, this charge is passed down from generation to generation. Wasn't death included with all the past generations?"

"Yeah for the most part, the fourth horseman doesn't live long. Often times, he's killed at birth. But for the last nine generations, we lost the family line. That's not the bad part. The bad part is a threat of the final horseman. He's a mean bastard with uncontrollable emotions. We fear that his wrath will hasten the apocalypse. He'll be the end of the world."

"Damn, should we be going to Houston?" Mallory joked. Matthew threw his head back. "I'm kidding. One joke I'm sorry." Mallory rolled his eyes. "So, does this final horseman know that you're after him?"

"I don't think so. He hasn't made his final conversion. He has missed many occasions to convert. That's another reason why it's so hard to find him. Most horsemen convert between the ages of 18-22."

"So how do you know that he hasn't converted?"

"There are studies out there that show that people are living longer than usual."

"Why go after him?"

"He's a living time bomb who can blow up at any moment. Just because he hasn't converted doesn't mean that he can't kill. He can get so angry that he can command one soul to leave a body and join his. That's how he survives, by consuming souls."

"If you find this Final, what would you do?"

"He needs to be neutralized. I'm going to kill him." Matthew commanded harshly.

"You would kill him? You?" Mallory asked sharply. Matthew nodded with no hesitation. "That's brutal."

"Emerald, he's the end of the world. You have to save humanity." Mallory bit his tongue hard and Matthew could see his jaw clenching. "What?"

"I'm not saying anything. I promised an open mind." He said clenching his teeth. "Could you really kill him?"

"No hesitation."

"Well, damn! I learn something new every day. I hope it's not me. May your God be on your side. Damn, the way you look right now ... I don't think that I want to go up against you."

"Well, it's nice to know that I could look threatening."

"Threatening or horny, either one." They both laughed. Mallory grabbed his hand and they started singing as he turned off the highway, heading toward Houston.

CHAPTER SEVEN

Not long after Matthew arrived back in Jerusalem, Mallory received an invitation to visit him. Against strong opposition from Peter, Mallory packed his bags and had his crew file a flight plan. His brothers were pressuring him to join the company, and he had had just about enough of them. He needed to get away. He figured, who better to get away with than Matthew.

As Mallory stepped off his leer jet with anticipation, the harsh sun blinded him briefly. He feverishly hunted for his sunglasses. Once he recovered his focus, he walked off the jet to see a car waiting. When he crawled into the car, a bouquet of cold bottled waters wrapped with purple ribbon greeted him with a note: *"Hey Emerald, thanks for coming."*

"Mr. Peterson is waiting for you at the site, sir," the driver said.

"Please take me to the hotel first. This arid climate is killing me," Mallory instructed.

The dig site was many miles outside the city. Mallory watched the landscape rise and fall through the dark tint of the windows. He did not see what Matthew found so appealing about the countryside, but he was willing to keep an open mind. When his car arrived to the site, he stepped out prepared with his sunglasses on this time. He strolled slowly through the site inspecting different artifacts and scrolls. He noticed the workers had stopped in their tracks and strangely watched his every move, as if they feared him. It bothered him a bit, but he gave their behavior no particular attention.

His attention fell upon a long, steel double-edged sword shining in the sun. He bent down to study the detailing in the pearl handle and the sharpness of the edges. As he went to touch the sword, a high-pitched sound rang out.

Mallory shielded his ears from the ominous sound. Soon, the pitch leveled off and vibrations of the humming captivated him. The sword was calling him — his palms ached, begging him to touch it. When he reached out, the sword levitated and flew to him. Mallory fell back onto the ground and the sword dropped at his feet. He jumped up and dusted himself off, walking away quickly.

As he strolled down another sandy pathway, a painted black glass horse statue captured his attention. He studied the detailing and its unique design. The gold beaded rope around the horse's neck began rotating, and the horse dipped his head. Mallory was fascinated, as the miniature horse came to life before his eyes. The horse turned his head, facing him, and the emerald jeweled eyes started glowing. It startled him. He shook his head and then walked away quickly.

Matthew spotted him and rushed in his direction. When he reached Mallory, he embraced him strongly, taking him by surprise.

"How do they feel about gay people?" Mallory asked.

"I don't care! Give me a kiss." Matthew planted a hard smack on Mallory's lips.

Mallory grabbed his waist and kissed him but became interrupted when a small sand storm disrupted their affections. "Get me out of this sand, it's cutting me."

Matthew grabbed his hand, "Follow me, silly. We're going into the cave."

"Cave? I'm not going into a bloody cave." Mallory jerked his hand back.

"Emerald, it's structurally sound."

"I don't care. You know that I'm claustrophobic."

"You were homophobic at one time, and you got over that." Matthew snatched his hand and pulled him to follow. Once they reached the entrance to the cave, Mallory saw ancient drawings scrawled on each side of the walls and scrolls laying everywhere.

Mallory also noticed a rope on both sides of the walkway. "What's this for?" He went to touch the rope.

"Oh, I forgot to tell you. Stay on the path and don't reach over. That's holy ground." Matthew pointed on both sides.

"Holy ground?" Mallory asked sarcastically.

"Yes, holy ground. Don't test it."

"I won't if you say so." Mallory looked worried. As they walked, Mallory looked at the cave walls. The drawings on the walls were of ancient pictures that told a story.

Mallory took note of a scene of a man in black walking out of smoke and ash. "Have I seen this before?" Mallory tried hard recalling where he had seen this painting. Although the drawings were faded, he could see the pained expressions on the faces. He shook his head and moved on.

As he continued to follow Matthew deep in the cave, the ring on his left finger began aching. When Matthew turned back, he saw Mallory tugging and fighting with the ring.

"What wrong with your finger?"

"It feels like it's squeezing my finger off. I can't adjust it or take it off."

"Yeah, mine does that too sometimes. It's the heat. Just shake it off."

As they walked, Mallory noticed that the rope stopped and the sand pathway gave way to rich green grass. He paused for a moment before he took a step. He saw Matthew walk on the grass with no hesitation. But when he stepped on the grass, the ground started trembling. "You trying to bloody kill me?"

"Watch your mouth!" Matthew hissed. "There are monks in here."

"What's happening, Matty?" He stepped back on the sandy pathway.

"I don't know. It's been a while since this happened."

"Well, I need to get out of here." Mallory started walking back.

"Just wait. We'll be there in just a few steps. Give me your hand." He grabbed Mallory's hand and walked him over the threshold. "There are some people I want you to meet."

"Who are they?"

"A couple of professors and some monks." He stood back and pushed Mallory toward the exhibit. Mallory looked down at the old parchment with ancient scribble, which didn't impress him much. He had seen many ancient scrolls in museums. But when he looked over at Matthew, he saw the beam of excitement in his eyes; he disguised his boredom. "Look, we found this scroll. No one here knows how to translate ancient Hebrew, so we're waiting for a linguist."

"Hebrew is easy."

"You know ancient Hebrew?"

"I know all languages." Mallory said that with such arrogance that Matthew was amazed.

"Okay, will you read this to me?" Matthew responded, matching his arrogant tone. He knew Mallory was a scholar, but knowing all languages meant Mallory would have been in school a long time.

"What will you do for me?"

"I'll cut this trip by a day."

"Just a day?"

"Emerald!"

"Fine." Mallory examined at it.

"Don't touch it."

"I won't."

Matthew pulled out a notepad and pen. "Okay, I'm ready."

"It says '*Let it be known ... that the final fourth shall explode as ... a thunderous cloud.*'"

"Really?"

"No! I'm making this shit up," he responded sarcastically. "Now stop talking, I'm trying to concentrate. I haven't read Hebrew in a while." He bent down to read the scroll. As he examined the document, the monks appeared. "' *The final is unproductive? An unproductive man ... born not of woman.*' You got that?"

"Yeah."

"What does that mean?"

"I'll figure it out later."

"'*Unproductive man ... born not of woman ... with pale face and piercing eyes and skin of ice.*'" Mallory was having a hard time reading the scrolls with his sunglasses on, so he took them off. When his glaring ice aquamarines appeared from the dark lens, the monks became outraged. They snatched the scroll from his reach and huddled in a corner screaming and praying. "What the bloody hell?"

"I don't know. What did you do? Did you touch it?"

"No! You told me not to touch it!" Mallory glared at the monks. They were screaming and shouting to each other in their native tongue. "They are saying that I'm not supposed to be in here. Do I need to leave?"

"Wait a minute," Matthew walked over to calm to monks and find out the problem.

The professor walked over and saw Mallory's glowing eyes. He was horror-stricken.

"Hi," He managed to get a word out of his mouth.

"Cheers?" Mallory frowned.

"How did you get in here?"

Mallory's finger began aching and he nervously tugged at the ring again. "I walked in with him," he pointed at Matthew.

"Okay?" The professor bowed his head in horror, which Mallory found strange. "Matthew, can I talk to you for a moment?"

"Yeah. What's going on? Why are they acting this way?"

"Can he leave the cave?" The professor's voice shook with nervousness.

"You don't have to ask me twice, I'm leaving now." Mallory turned around and began walking out of the cave before Matthew could answer.

When he stepped over the threshold, he felt a slight tremor and saw two pathways. *"Always take the right hand side."* He proceeded to walk down the path to the right. He turned back and took the left path. *"He would be judging me so it would be His right hand."* As he took long strides out of the cave, he slowed down when he saw a crystal white waterfall flowing down the wall. *"That wasn't here before."*

"Why did you bring him in here?" the professor fussed.

"What's the big deal? He's my boyfriend. I told you he was coming. We've had visitors before. Besides, he was helping us translate this," he defended Mallory's presence. "What's wrong?"

Mallory got closer to the stream and a cool breeze from the waterfall whipped across his face. Mallory closed his eyes and inhaled the peacefulness of the falling water. He remembered that he wasn't supposed to touch the rope. But when he opened his eyes to gauge where he was standing; the stream of water turned bloody and violently lunged at him.

"Matthew, that's your boyfriend?" the professor shouted. "Oh God, do you know what you have done? Do you know what he is?"

Matthew looked in Mallory's direction but couldn't see him.

"Matthew, he is —"

Just then, Mallory fell back in a panic and landed on the other side, breaking the rope. The ground began shaking violently.

"Shit, I need to go get him." Matthew ran down the path toward Mallory and found him on the ground struggling to get up. The more he struggled, the more the rope entangled his body. He couldn't get a good grasp to sit up. "Emerald, give me your hand."

"Matthew, do you see this? This ground is disappearing."

"Emerald, focus baby. Give me your hand. Don't touch the ground! Just give me your hand."

"It's disappearing!"

Using his left hand, Matthew managed to grab Mallory's left hand and the rings touched. The ground trembled harder and they both fell over. Mallory's head landed on the holy ground. He saw the ground disappear and his body floated over an abyss. "Get me up, please!" he screamed.

"Okay, hold on!"

The professor ran over to rescue Matthew. He struggled but finally managed to lift Matthew up off the ground. Once Matthew got solid footing, he attempted to grab for Mallory.

The professor held him back. "NO! Let him die!"

"Hell no!" Matthew grabbed Mallory's right hand. As he lifted Mallory up, When Mallory touched the cave wall, the trembling grew ferociously and then the wall began burning.

"Let's get out of here, baby."

They all ran out just before the cave entrance collapsed.

"Damn! Are you okay, Emerald?" Matthew looked at the destruction of the cave.

"No!" Mallory screamed out, holding his burning hand. He kept rubbing his hand against his clothes as if he was trying to put out a fire.

Matthew turned toward him brushing the sand off his clothes and examining him closely. "What's wrong?" He noticed Mallory rubbing his hand but couldn't understand why.

Mallory looked down at his hand. It appeared to look normal but it was still burning. "I'm fine."

"Let me take you back to the hotel."

The professor snatched Matthew's arm. "Matthew, we need to talk."

"Look, I'll be back. I just need to see if he's okay."

"No, you don't."

"Yes, I do."

"NO! You need to stop protecting —" The professor shouted but stopped short when Mallory glared at him with his piercing eyes. The professor bowed his head in fear, confusing Mallory even more.

"Look, I just need to take him to the hotel," Matthew explained to the professor. "I'll be back, okay?"

"Be careful," the professor warned him.

"I'll be fine," Matthew said as he grabbed Mallory's arm and rushed him to the car. He slammed the door and the driver peeled off. Matthew grabbed a cold bottle of water and handed it to Mallory. He grabbed the bottle with his left hand, and the plastic melted, spilling water on the floor.

"Shit!" Mallory said as he dropped the bottle.

"Sorry? Take this one."

Mallory grabbed it with his right hand and opened the bottle but didn't take a drink. Matthew frantically opened his bottle and practically finished it in three gulps. They both took deep breaths. Mallory laid his head back. Sunrays escaped through the cracks of the tinted glass and beamed directly into Mallory's eyes. The constant squinting gave him a headache. "My sunglasses are in the cave."

"Your sunglasses?" Matthew wanted to interrogate him and found the perfect opportunity.

"I took them off when I was trying to read that scroll. Them bloody fucking monks..."

"What happened? What did you do?" Matthew grilled him further.

"Nothing! I was reading the scroll and things were fine until I took them off and then they just went bloody bonkers!"

"I wondered why?" Matthew sat back and closed his eyes.

"I think I want to go home."

"I know you do baby, go home tomorrow." He grabbed Mallory's hand. "I wanna spend the night with you."

"Then I'll leave tomorrow. EARLY!" Mallory said. He finally found a position away from the sunrays and laid his head back, again closing his eyes. He kept rubbing his left hand, which cooled off a bit but continued aching. The words of the scroll burned in his eyelids.

"Unproductive man, born not of woman. With a pale face, piercing eyes and skin of ice."

The next line appeared to Mallory.

"He was born with a tortured soul and uncontrollable emotions. His greatest love is his —"

Mallory squeezed his eyes trying to translate that last word on the scroll, but he drew a blank. He opened his eyes and down at Matthew who was lying in his lap asleep. He didn't want to disturb him.

"I'll tell him later."

Matthew crawled out of the shower and flopped on the bed next to Mallory. He was so confused and exhausted. He knew Mallory had a lot of criticizing questions and condescending comments. Matthew wasn't in the mood for one of his tirades. As they looked at each other, they were speechless.

Mallory wanted to share his dogma about false beliefs. Moreover, that God, if there was a God, doesn't kill people; people, and poor sound structures, kill people. Instead of arguing, he grabbed Matthew softly and brought him over, holding him close to his chest. Matthew tried to find comfort in him by circling Mallory's chest with his fingertips but he felt strange being with him. Nevertheless, he wanted to feel his touch.

After a while, Matthew finally sat up and asked, "Would you mind if we didn't have sex tonight?"

"Yes I would mine," Mallory said sternly. "Are you hungry?" He caressed his chin and kissed his forehead.

"Yeah, but I don't wanna go out."

"That's why they have room service love," Mallory said sarcastically as he grabbed the menu.

"What would I do without you?" Matthew replied sarcastically.

"What's wrong?"

"Do you ever get the feeling that something is staring you in the face, but you don't see it?"

"No."

"You know, like everybody knows something that you're supposed to know but you don't ..." Matthew tried to explain himself but he kept getting frustrated because he couldn't find the right words. Mallory just shook his head. "Never mind."

"Look, I know that you're upset about today. I shouldn't have come. Peter told me not to."

"That's just it. Why didn't he want you to come?"

"I don't know, but he was pissed about it. I think he's unhappy with the homosexual relationship. I love Peter, but if he makes me choose, he's gone."

"I think it's more than that."

"Well, I don't care. I only care to see that you're well fed and fucked. At this point, you're neither."

"Emerald," he snickered. "Order me something ... anything."

Mallory picked up the phone with the menu in the other hand.

"And bring your sexy ass over here."

"I thought you said no?"

"I changed my mind."

"This is earth shattering! Should I get off the phone before you change it back?"

"No, you know you have a way of making me say yes. Especially when sex is concerned."

After Mallory ordered room service, he slammed the phone down and crawled on Matthew. He started with his calves, kissing and biting him all over. Matthew closed his eyes absorbing Mallory's touch, but when he opened his eyes, he noticed a white cloud growing in the room. He looked down at Mallory, who was too preoccupied to notice it. He called out to Mallory, but he wouldn't look up. Mallory grabbed his penis and started kissing and tonguing it.

The white cloud grew wider and consumed everything it touched. Matthew tried harder to get Mallory's attention by screaming his name but he wouldn't look up. The cloud reached the foot of the bed and started spreading. Everything it touched disappeared. The cloud finally reached Mallory's feet, but he still didn't notice it. As he enveloped Matthew's penis, the cloud covered him and he disappeared. Matthew screamed. "Emerald!" He woke up to a dark room. "Emerald, where are you? Didn't you hear me call you?"

Mallory sat up abruptly. "When?"

"I was just calling you. Didn't you see the cloud?"

"What cloud?" Mallory looked around the pitch-dark room.

"It was in the room, you were going down on me and the cloud ..."

"Are you off your tits? I went down on you? Right! I don't think so. The first thing you declared before took your shower is that you DID NOT want to have sex tonight."

"You didn't go down on me? You didn't order room service?"

"No. You said you weren't hungry. You kissed me on the forehead and turned over."

"Damn! Which one was the bad dream? The cloud or you not having sex with me?"

"I don't know anything about a cloud, Matty. But you know me ..." Mallory tucked his pillow and laid back down. "I'll get it in the morning."

"Okay, now I know I'm not dreaming." Matthew laid back down and tussled a bit before finding a comfortable spot to settle down. Lying on his stomach, he felt Mallory's fingertip running down his back. Soon he felt Mallory's weight covering him. "It must be morning." Mallory gradually kissed him down the spine of his back. "That feels so good."

Mallory finally made it to his neck and ears. He whispered, "I want you baby." Matthew wrapped his fingers around the edge of the mattress. When he opened his eyes, he noticed that he was lying on a billowy white cloud and everything around him was consumed by the cloud. He no longer felt Mallory's weight. He turned over and the cloud was enveloping him.

Matthew couldn't breathe as he grabbed his throat feverishly calling for Mallory. "EMERALD!" He violently woke up screaming his name. "Emerald, where are you?"

Mallory stepped out of the bathroom fully dressed, wiping his hands with a finger towel. "I'm right here. What the bloody hell is wrong with you?"

"Oh, Emerald. Tell me that we did it this morning."

"You ARE off your tits today! You were sleeping so hard, I wasn't about to wake you up. I got up, had breakfast and read the paper. I left some here for you." Mallory laid the towel on the counter and walked over to Matthew's side of the bed. "There is a story in the paper about the accident."

Matthew scratched his head in confusion. "Emerald, I'm going crazy. I could have sworn that you were on me."

"... and you could have sworn that I blew you last night." Mallory crawled in the bed, gently forcing Matthew to lie down.

"I think you would know if I was doing you. You wouldn't see anything else." He tried to kiss him but Matthew turned his head.

"Get up! I don't know if I'm dreaming or not and I don't wanna get into it and you disappear."

"I disappear?"

"Yeah, in a white cloud. This cloud comes and makes everything disappear." He looked up at Mallory.

Mallory positioned himself on him and slowly unzipped his pants. "Keep talking."

"The cloud consumes everything in the room and it gets me and I can't breath. I'm choking and I can't ... oh shit, that feels so good." Matthew closed his eyes.

"I told you baby... you wouldn't see anything else if I was inside you. Open your eyes, baby," Mallory said, gently biting his ears.

Matthew shook his head and clenched his eyes shut.

"You know I can fuck you where you will never close your eyes again."

Matthew opened his eyes focusing only on Mallory.

"See I haven't disappeared." Mallory started kissing his neck.

"You're right, baby," Matthew bit into his shoulder then looked over it and saw the cloud. "Get up! Get up, Emerald. It's the cloud. It's going to get you."

Mallory looked back, "There is nothing behind me."

"It's right there. Get up, get up please."

Mallory pulled out and sat up, "Where is it?"

"It's right there," Matthew fiercely pointed to an empty area in the room.

Mallory didn't feel like indulging his hallucinations. He cupped Matthew's pale face making him focus all his attention on him. "What's wrong, baby?" He looked deeply into Matthew's dark sunken eyes and saw that he was exhausted.

"I think I'm going crazy. It's haunting me," He managed to sit with Mallory in his lap.

"Is this the first time you've seen this cloud?"

"No, I see it every time I get ready to come home, but never this intense."

"That's it. You're working too hard. You're worn out and dehydrated. I'm taking you home." Mallory leaped off the bed and zipped his pants. He headed toward the closet and started pulling out Matthew's things.

"Emerald, I can't go."

"You thought that was a request?"

"Emerald, I have so much work to do."

"You're also breaking down. Let's just go home, just for a little while."

"No, Emerald. I can't."

Mallory pushed him back on the bed and leaned over him. "Do you honestly think you can win this argument with me in your condition?"

He looked deeply in Mallory's eyes. "No, baby. I need to make some phone calls."

Mallory pulled his cell phone from his pocket, placing it in his hand, and then started packing Matthew's things. Matthew called the head professor to inform him that was returning home for a while.

"Shit, it's too bloody hot here and I'm a cold-natured person. This place is worse than Houston. It's not like you have real AC.

No wonder you're having hallucinations," Mallory fussed as he threw Matthew's things in the bag.

Matthew hung up the phone and bowed his head trying to ignore Mallory's ranting. He finally crawled out of the bed and barely threw on a t-shirt and old jeans.

"Let's go. Maybe I'll make it back home for this big memorial." Mallory picked up the phone to call the concierge.

"What memorial?"

"Yours if we don't leave soon."

After several arguments, Mallory finally got Matthew to leave the hotel room. The professor kept calling Matthew, pleading with him not to leave and begging him to return to the dig site, but Mallory was adamant about taking Matthew home. Mallory finally turned the cell phone off and escorted a tired Matthew in the car.

When they reached the jet, Mallory jumped out and quickly handed the bags to the attendant, but Matthew crept out of the car. His strength was beyond spent and he was distressed. He knew that this was a bad time to leave, but Mallory was adamant about going home. Mallory grabbed his hand and they slowly ascended the stairs.

Matthew hesitated when he saw the cloud appear again. "Emerald, you don't see it?"

Mallory looked up in the sky. "There is not a bloody cloud in the sky."

"No, Emerald. It's blocking the entrance."

Mallory stood in front of him. "Look, I'm here. I'll let nothing harm you. Close your eyes and I'll guide you."

Matthew closed his eyes and Mallory guided him up each step. As he got higher, Matthew begin choking and grabbing his throat.

Mallory stopped and kissed him softly. "You're okay, baby. Your God is here and I'll protect you."

When Matthew opened his eyes, the cloud disappeared and he was relieved. Mallory resumed guiding him up the stairs. Matthew looked back and saw the cloud floating in the distance. He felt emptiness inside. Mallory pulled his hand and guided him to his seat.

"You'll be back soon. You just need to regroup and I need to take care of you."

CHAPTER EIGHT

Matthew stood in a long line at the airport counter, waiting to check in. As he waited, the desires of being with Mallory filled his mind. It was the anniversary of their first night as lovers. With each reminiscing thought, Matthew blushed and his arousal grew stronger. He wanted to surprise Mallory by coming home unannounced. He closed his eyes and imagined Mallory's face when he walked through the door.

Matthew finally made it to the front of the counter, when his daydream popped. "Sir, this fight is cancelled," the attendant said.

"Cancelled!" He slammed his hand on the counter. "Why?"

"Bad weather, sir."

"Damn!" He regained his composure. "When is the next flight?"

"Tomorrow maybe, it's too soon to tell."

"I need to be there tomorrow."

"I'm sorry, sir."

"Thank you," Matthew was disgusted. He threw his bags across the seat and flopped down. He covered his face and sighed heavily. *Get over this Matty, there will be other anniversaries.* He searched for his cell phone and dialed Mallory's number, waiting for an answer, but there was no answer. He gathered his things and walked out to the exit, attempting to call him again. *Maybe I can convince him to spend our anniversary by webcam. Boy, he would love that!* He got Mallory's voicemail again. "DAMN!" Matthew called the office, but Melody was vague and very cold.

As he stood outside contemplating his dilemma, he noticed that the driver who dropped him off at the airport was still there. He walked over and the driver opened the door for him.

"Back to the hotel, Mr. Peterson?" The driver gathered his bags and put them in the car.

"Yeah, I guess." Matthew shuffled into the car and threw his head back against the headrest. He was so disgusted. Two months had passed since they were together, and he really wanted to see Mallory.

"Sir, I have a message for you."

Matthew perked up. "A message?"

The driver handed him a disk.

Matthew pulled out his laptop and turned it on. "Hurry! Hurry!" Once the laptop booted up, the file started. Mallory created an electronic love-gram video for Matthew. Although he beamed inside, the gesture made him crave Mallory more. The car filled with melodies of Ginuwine's *So Anxious*.

Mallory recorded himself singing a song that fit his personality perfectly. The video started with an empty chair, and then Mallory appeared wearing dark sunglasses and a black suit, straddling the chair, positioning a glass of wine and the latest version on Matthew's favorite E Lynn Harris book on the table.

Matthew could hardly contain his excitement as Mallory moved his body perfectly to the rhythm. He finally realized how Mallory felt every time he sent those love songs. He leaned back in his seat and strategically placed the laptop on his crotch, enjoying his electronic lap dance. He lip-synched the verses while watching Mallory dance erotically and strip. Every piece of clothing he took off was thrown at the camera, and Matthew pretended to catch it, biting his lip. Matthew agreed when Mallory sang, "... *Boy, could you quit this stalling. You know that I'm a sexaholic.*"

Before the bridge of the song, Mallory stood wearing only a black mesh thong. The song kept playing but he disappeared behind the camera leaving a sign on the chair stating, "*To be continued ...*" Seconds later, the thong landed on the camera. Matthew wanted to jump through the laptop and take a bite out of Mallory. Even better, he wanted to get to a webcam as soon he could. He had a couple of ideas he wanted to send to Mallory. Just then, the driver turned left, driving away from the hotel.

"No I need to go back to the hotel." Matthew shouted.

"I understand, sir, but I have strict instructions to take you to the private hangar before 11:30 and I'm late because I was waiting for you. He told me to tell you to listen to the words."

A smile exploded on Matthew's face as he leaned back and replayed the video. The driver finally pulled up to the jet and Matthew jumped out of the car, leaving all his belongings behind. When he saw Mallory sitting on the stairs, Matthew ran up the stairs and stopped short of him.

"It's midnight and you're late." Mallory said.

"Traffic," He leaned down to kiss him.

"You think we can fuck here?"

"On the stairs?" Matthew scrunched his nose and shook his head. "That would hurt worst than carpet burn."

"But I'm so anxious," He licked his lips and leaned back further on the steps. Matthew walked up a couple of steps. Mallory grabbed Matthew's zipper with his teeth. Matthew held out his hands and helped him up.

"Come baby, take me home."

"I can't. Bloody hurricane is hitting Texas."

"How did you know I was coming?"

"You can't keep anything from me, I'm your God." He teased but Matthew didn't find it funny. "Besides, Melody told me you used my credit card." Mallory gloated but Matthew shook his head. "Can I see my present?"

"No. I can't believe them son of bitches cut off my expense card." Matthew rolled his eyes. "I guess they got my notice that I quit the company."

"I'll wait," Mallory kissed him on the cheek. "I have a surprise for you."

"I'm listening."

"We're going to Amsterdam," Mallory kissed him again.

"Oh baby!"

"I even got the room we had the first time."

"That single bed?" Matthew frowned.

"Absobloodylutely," he chuckled. "No baby, not the way we do it now, but I thought about it."

As they settled in their hotel suite, Mallory gathered the champagne and fruit and brought them to the bath suite. He drew a hot bath then settled in the tub, pouring two glasses of champagne and nibbled on some fruit. He eagerly waited for Matthew, who was shuffling around a bit before finally joining him in the tub.

"What have you been doing?" Mallory asked impatiently.

"I needed to make some phone calls. How bad is the hurricane?" Matthew said, settling in and adding more hot water. He finally nestled under Mallory and handed him a box.

"Bad enough that I had to stay in New York for a night if I wanted to get out." Mallory opened the box and saw a delicate silver chain with a pendant. It was a uniquely shaped crucifix. Mallory looked at him strangely, "A cross?"

"Not just a cross? It's special. Read the back."

Mallory turned it over and read the back. "To my higher power," then he looked at him again for explanation.

"You are my God, my higher power, my blessing. I honor you, protect your name, and worship you always. I'll sacrifice anything for you." Matthew held his hands up. "You're my omnipotent. No one above you."

"That's sounds like a wedding vow," Mallory sadly uttered.

"You can take it as such." He grabbed the chain and placed it on Mallory's neck. He kissed the crucifix, then Mallory's lips. Matthew turned around and laid back on Mallory's chest. "I designed it myself, and then found a jeweler to make it for me. It took him two weeks. I thought I wasn't gonna get it back in time. When I had to use your credit card, I figured you would find out."

"You know I don't look at my credit card bills. That's why I have Melody." Mallory ran his fingertips up his leg. "Damn, I didn't get you anything."

"You got me here."

"But this looks last minute."

"That's okay, Emerald. We're here together." Matthew grabbed his arms, wrapped them around his body and started to rock. Their song, *Make Me a Believer* by Luther Vandross, played on the laptop and they began swaying to the beat. Matthew started singing. Mallory closed his eyes, cupping his hand and pouring water on Matthew's exposed body.

"You sang this to me at the lake. The first time we really made love ... and I didn't throw up."

Matthew nodded as he nestled his head on Mallory's chest. He closed his eyes and continued singing.

Mallory poured more water on his body and occasionally ran his fingertips across Matthew's thigh and continued singing the rest of the song. He couldn't wait any longer, so he grabbed a little bag from the side of the tub and handed it to Matthew. He unwrapped the box and pulled out a sterling silver Rado watch with 48 diamonds in the face. He flashed his pearly whites toward Mallory.

"Read the back," Mallory said.

"There is only one power and one presence in my life," Matthew read. He turned to Mallory, "You didn't forget."

"You know I can't forget our day... the day that changed my life forever." He placed the watch on Matthew's wrist.

Matthew sat back and entangled his hand with Mallory's and the watch dipped in the water.

"Now don't get it wet."

"Shut up. It can handle a little water," They swayed to the rest of the song. The song ended but they laid in each other's arms until a chill woke them up from a light slumber. Matthew jumped out of the tub. "This water is getting cold. Let's get out." Matthew grabbed the towel and dried Mallory's back. When he walked out, Mallory popped him with the towel. "Alright bitch."

"I couldn't refuse," Mallory teased.

"Okay, I'll refuse you tonight."

"You'll refuse to please your God," he shouted with authority.

"Pop me again with the fucking towel, and I'll show you what I can refuse."

"'Blasphemy!" Mallory tackled Matthew and they fell on the bed. They wrestled a bit and Mallory started nibbling on his neck. Matthew decided to stop wrestling and allow Mallory's warm tongue to explore his body. Mallory finally reached his face and they gazed in each other's eyes. "Do you think we will feel like this forever?"

"No." Matthew laughed. "Hell I don't know. I don't want to think about that. I just want to enjoy you now."

Mallory sat up looking as if he wanted to confess.

"What's up, Emerald?"

He looked down, rubbing his face. "I guess I always confess before we make love."

"Like a true servant," Matthew teased.

"I ... uh ... found out what I need to do ... for the proselytization."

"What? A live cow?" he joked.

"No a virgin?" Mallory didn't smile.

Matthew almost fell off the bed laughing. "Well that's right up your old alley."

"No, Matty. I have to get married and she must be a virgin."

"Now where are they going to find one of those, especially for you?"

"I don't know. I haven't gotten over the fact that I have to be married."

"I don't understand ... to be a part of the company, you have to be married. Shit, marry me," Matthew said.

"I thought about that, but before I could get it out of my mouth, Malcolm yelled 'Hell No!'"

"Doesn't he know this is the new millennium? States are approving same-sex marriages now," Matthew asked and Mallory nodded. "Is he still mad about the heart attack?"

Mallory nodded again.

"That'll teach him to come in my office at night."

Mallory fell back in the bed and looked at the ceiling fan. "What would you do if you saw your two boys fucking on the desk?"

"Close the damn door, not have a bloody heart attack and fall to the fucking floor." Matthew laughed harder.

"That's not funny. We almost killed Malcolm. As many times as I wanted him to die —that way never crossed my mind."

"You should have seen his face when I went to give him mouth to mouth ..." Matthew couldn't finish the statement.

"Shit, I still can't listen to Ray Charles. I'm shell shocked." Mallory covered his face with a pillow. "I think something is weird about him lately. He has been very distant... even like an absentee."

Matthew controlled his laughter. "What do you mean?"

"After that memorial...he has this guilty look."

"That Luxapher memorial? They had a private funeral, then a long and weird three-month memorial for the guy. It was like we were paying homage to a God. Did you know him?"

"Not personally. I think they are family friends. He was a Lord or Emperor. Anyway, Malcolm just seemed guilty like...I can't explain it."

"Forget that for a moment, explain the virgin?"

"I don't know. That's strange, too. I really just want to get out of it. I mean you're here now. I don't need this. But I signed a letter of intent and if I forfeit, they take my company and all my assets."

"Shit! Really?" Matthew sat up and asked. "You're calm about this."

"Oh boy, that hurricane that's hitting Texas right now can't compare to the fury I feel. I'm just sick. I had to leave. I don't know what to do. I have my attorney looking in it."

"No other options?"

"I have options. I can start over." Mallory sat up and grabbed his hand. "That's why I asked if we could feel this way forever … well not forever … but for awhile."

"Yeah, Emerald, we have been this way for awhile. But that's your baby. You fathered Towneson Financial. You can't give that up. I know how much you love your company."

"I know but I would give it up for you."

"Damn. Talk about your sacrifices." He crawled over to Mallory and grabbed his body.

Mallory laid his head on his shoulder. "Tell me what to do… I'll do anything that you want. I need to decide something soon."

"You don't have to decide tonight," Matthew said as he climbed in front of Mallory. "We'll decide in the morning. Tonight, you need to decide how you want it." Mallory leaned back and pulled Matthew on top of him, "Happy anniversary baby."

CHAPTER NINE

Melody and Natasha were at the receptionist desk, talking when Mallory walked to the front office. He saw that they were enthralled in a deep conversation. Mallory hated office gossip, especially if he was the topic of discussion. He knew Melody would never give intimate details of any of his outrageous behavior, but she was great at spreading what she heard. He moved closer, trying not to make any noise. Melody's expression and body language told Mallory that this news was hot and juicy.

He held his breath and moved closer, when he heard Melody say loudly, "Gurl, and then the monkey said to the hunter – I'll shoot you in the ass if you walk up behind me like that." The two women laughed, but Mallory didn't find the humor. "You can hold your breath and tiptoe around here all you want; we can smell you a mile away with that expensive cologne you wear."

"HA HA!" he snapped. "Who are you two talking about?"

"Not you! You ain't worth a quarter to talk about." She turned to Natasha, "Now, his brother, oh that dark pot licker chocolate boy. Now he's something to talk about."

"Marek?" Mallory rolled his eyes.

"Oh, Marek. Now the sound of that name makes me want to take my heart medicine," she grunted. Natasha smiled but didn't respond because she wanted to stay out of this conversation. "Is he married?"

"Happily!" Mallory rolled his eyes. "Speaking of which, I'm expecting a visitor. Her name is Stacy Silverman. When she gets here, can you call me?"

"Who is Stacy?" Melody asked.

"Some arranged date."

"You have arranged dates now? I told you that being with Matthew would fuck up your game."

"When did you tell me that, Bold Betty?"

"Well I thought it. Besides, what do you need an arrangement for? You're in a relationship with that gay blade."

"Why do you hate Matthew?"

"I don't hate the boy. I just hate your little nasty ways. You two ashy ass men laying up next to each —"

"I'm well-groomed. There is not one bit of ash on me!" Mallory interrupted her.

"Don't back talk me, boy! Now like I said, you don't need a man doing that nasty shit. All you need is a good woman and a stick."

"Natasha, I'm going to need a replacement soon. When do you get out of grad school?"

"In two years, sir."

"Replace my ass if you want to. You will walk in here one day and won't be able to find your brain between your two scrotums."

"I'm not talking to you anymore," He turned to Natasha. "Just tell me when Stacy gets here. Thank you."

"I will, sir." Natasha grinned and watched Mallory walk back to his office. "Aunt Melody, why are you so hard on him?"

"I hate when a good man go bad. Shoot, I had plans for that boy. Whew someone needs to knock down his God complex. You know, that boy thinks he's Zeus."

"More like Apollo ..." Natasha said under her breath, "with his sexy body."

"Natasha, when she comes, you call me. I need to check this hoecake out. She may be a transvestite."

Natasha laughed.

"It's true. It's bad enough that they don't think when they sticking us, but when they sticking themselves, they just go stupid."

Natasha laughed so hard that she could barely sit in her chair.

When Stacy walked into Towneson Financial, no one was at the front desk. She walked toward the offices, most of which were empty because it was lunchtime. She didn't want to ask anyone where Mallory's office was, so she roamed around. When she reached the end of the hall, she saw an open office door. She walked slowly toward the door and looked at the engraved plaque: *Mallory Towneson*.

She saw Mallory at his desk, working hard and swaying to his music. He had earphones in and didn't notice her. She studied him intensely. He had an intense but friendly face, looking mature but not old. When he bit his lip, she saw his perfectly polished pearly white teeth. Every once and a while, he broke out in a chorus and she laughed. At one point, he closed his eyes and sang loudly.

He opened his eyes and jumped. "Oh shit. Who the bloody hell are you?"

"I am ..."

"What are you doing here? Looking for your parent?" he shouted.

"NO! I am ... Stacy ... Stacy Silverman."

"Who?"

"Stacy."

Mallory tried to compose him. "You are Stacy Silverman? Senator Silverman's daughter?"

"Yes."

"Have a seat." Mallory sighed. "Do you want some milk or something?"

"No."

"Okay...Melody!" He shouted.

Melody rushed in, "Why are you hollarin'?"

"This is Stacy. Can you take her somewhere for a moment? I need to make a quick phone call."

When Melody escorted her out, Mallory rushed to the phone and called Marc's office. His assistant answered, so he slammed the phone down. "I can't stand that bitch." He picked up the phone again to dial Marek's phone number and his assistant answered. "Hi ..." He couldn't remember her name. "This is Mallory. Is Marek around?"

"Yes, they're all in his office."

"Can I speak to him please?"

She transferred the call to Marek's office. "MT what's up?" Marek said, putting Mallory on speaker.

"She's three! Fucking three years old," Mallory shouted.

"No she ain't," he laughed. "She's nineteen."

"This is rubbish. So what, I'm a pedophile now?"

They all laughed. "Marek, get me off the bloody speaker or I will talk!"

Marek jerked the phone up. "What bitch?"

"I'm glad that I can be a healthy dose for your amusement."

"Chill out muthafucka, she's legal."

"Barely! I like for my wife to be able to drink at the wedding. This girl is three!"

"Don't worry man. You'll be alright. Ain't that many 30-year-old virgins out there... and the ones who are out there, I don't think you want. Yo' know your ass so particular."

"This is crazy," he looked outside his door and spotted Stacy storming out of the office. "Oh, I gotta go." He slammed the phone down and trotted off to catch her. "Stacy...wait! Stacy!"

She walked through the double glass doors and reached the elevator.

"Stacy, wait!"

She turned to him and shouted, "Look, I'm not three. I'm nineteen. I don't think it's fair that I have to marry a fucking 40-year-old man."

"I'm not forty."

"You look forty," she shouted.

"I don't look forty! I don't even look thirty," he snapped back.

"You still look old."

Mallory took a deep breath. "Okay, maybe I deserved that. Come back in please? Please?"

She hesitated but decided to walk back into the office with him.

"Look, I promised you lunch, wherever you want to go."

She didn't respond. They walked back into the office and Melody was there waiting.

Mallory mouthed a threat to her, "not a word from you." She looked down trying not to laugh. He grabbed his keys and coat, and then called down to the garage. He turned toward Stacy and studied her a bit. She was a beautiful little teenager, standing 5-7, a medium caramel color and very shapely for her age. Her hips were very much defined. He could see that she was uncomfortable in her white halter-top tailored suit, as she struggled standing in her black and white 3-inch strappy heels.

"Why didn't she just wear jeans and a T-shirt?"

Her hair was pulled in a bun, but he could tell that it was wavy long brown with blonde streaks. She was definitely uncomfortable, and he made the situation worse when she overheard his juvenile conversation with Marek.

"Well, where would you like to eat?" He wanted to suggest McDonald's but thought it might exacerbate the situation.

"Madeline's," she maturely repeated the rehearsed response.

"Brilliant."

They arrived at the garage and he motioned to the attendant that he would open her door. She paused for a second, and then got in. She was silent during the entire drive. When they reached the parking lot to the restaurant, Mallory grabbed her hand and told her, "I'll get the door." He walked over and opened her door.

She got out and pouted, "Is there a child safety lock on it?"

"No, I was being chivalrous. That shit is dead in your generation." Mallory snapped back but she stormed off before he finished. "This is not going to work." As they entered the restaurant and toward the counter, Mallory asked, "Do you know what you want to order?"

"I can order for myself, thank you."

"Fine! I just wanted to let you know that they don't have kids' menus here."

"Are you worried about money? If so, you can save money using the senior citizen discount you qualify for."

"Ouch."

"Can I help you?" the attendant asked from behind the counter.

"Yes, I would like a grilled chicken Caesar salad and a cup of tomato basil soup," Stacy answered with another rehearsed response.

"That sounds brilliant. I'll have the same, except I want a bowl of soup," he said with a smile, but she just rolled her eyes. He wanted to carry her tray for her, but he knew that would send her over the edge in anger.

"Drinks?"

"Diet Coke."

"Can I get a white wine?" Mallory asked the attendant politely.

"You drink this early?"

"It's afternoon."

"Okay wino," she snarled, as she grabbed her tray then stormed off again.

The attendant handed Mallory the bill and asked him, "What's wrong with her?"

"First date," he smiled. He walked toward the table that she picked, which was in the middle of the restaurant. Mallory wanted some place more secluded, but he was not going to ask her to move. She finally decided to take off her jacket. He admired her innocently. "I like your suit."

"Thank you. It's my mother's," she said coldly.

"She has great taste."

"It sucks."

"Okay, it sucks on you but its still a cute suit."

"Fuck you, old man."

"What the hell is wrong with you?"

"I don't think it's fair that I have to give up being happy to marry your old faggot ass!" she shouted.

"You're a little terror tubby bitch, aren't you?"

"And you're a faggot!" she screamed out and stormed out of the restaurant.

Mallory sat there covering his face in embarrassment. It wasn't the fact that she called him names in public, but because she was hurt and he couldn't comfort her. He decided to go after her. As he went out, he spotted her down the street, so he started running after her. He wanted to call her name but he knew that would antagonize her more and she would run faster.

He finally caught up with her and grabbed her arm. "Look, you can choose to be an adult here and tell me what's wrong."

Tears streaming down her eyes, she cried out, "I was studying piano at Juilliard. I was happy. They made me come home to marry you. You don't even like women."

"How do you know what I like?"

"Your brothers told me."

"Oh ... did my brothers tell you that I don't want to be married, either. Did they tell you that I'm forced to get married too? Did they?" He jerked her arm. "Look I'm not a desperate man. If I wanted to be married, I could have been at least fifty times over. And as far as that faggot shit," he paused, "I'm in love with him. I made a commitment to him and he's very important to me. Do you think I want to give him up for you? You don't even know me but you have judged and sentenced me." He stopped because he saw that his words made no impression on her. "Look, let's start over. I know you don't like Madeline's and I know you're uncomfortable in that bloody suit. Maybe if you can be yourself, we can enjoy this day, aye?" He huffed and released her arm. "What's your favorite place?"

"The mall," she wiped her tears.

"Then the mall it is." He walked her to the car and allowed her to open the car door. "I'll be right back," he walked back into the restaurant to retrieve her jacket. He paused for a moment then grabbed his glass of wine and chugged it down. He wiped his mouth and returned to the car. He got in the car to find Stacy fumbling with his stereo.

"Oh sorry."

"No worries. Find a song you like."

"All your CDs are of old people." She flipped to one song. "Isn't he dead?"

I'll never tease Matthew's about his gay songs again, he screamed silently. "I think there is something in there that's fairly new."

"You don't listen to rap?"

"Yes, but they're loaded in one of my trucks."

"Trucks? How many do you have?"

"As many as I want."

"Why?"

"I'm a faggot, remember? My automobiles must match my wardrobe," He smiled at himself and gave her a look to let her know that it was okay to laugh. She released a faint smile.

"Oh D'Angelo...he has a beautiful voice and his body is so sexy."

"I don't know about a sexy body, but he has a nice voice."

"You're not attracted to him?"

"No! I'm not attracted to men, just Matthew."

"Really? Taye Diggs, Morris Chestnut? Denzel ... everybody's attracted to Denzel."

"Not me. Give me Alicia Keys, Beyonce or Kelly ... oh Kelly. Shit J-Lo. Now I can rock her hips. Don't have me think about her," he shivered.

"So why are you with this Matthew?"

"We have a special relationship. It's not just sexual ... it's like an eternal connection. He provides things...feelings ... that I haven't felt with anybody else."

"Oh, so you're a down lower?"

"No!" He laughed. "I haven't slept with a woman since I have been with him."

"I guess that's intense."

"Yes, it is. So tell me about you? You play the piano."

"Yeah, I have been playing since I was three," she said proudly then cut her eyes when he snickered. "So, what, you're going to say I have been playing since yesterday?"

"No, I'm not making fun of your age anymore. You fight dirty. You called me a faggot in public."

"Sorry."

"That's okay. I'll get over it. I just won't go to that restaurant again."

They spent hours in the mall, shopping and eating at various fast food spots. He thought he bought her the perfect outfit that suited her age, but after seeing her in a pair of low-rise ripped jeans that hugged her hips perfectly and a baby T-shirt that blasted *Taking Applications* across her voluptuous bosom; he felt that it was a bad idea. At least in her mom's suit, he wasn't attracted to her. She undid her bun and her wavy locks fell down her back. *Alicia Keys looks with J-Lo hips was not a good combination.* Mallory thought as he ordered another smoothie to calm his urges.

As they walked, he spotted a piano in the middle of the mall. "If I asked you to do something, would you do it?"

"It depends."

"I would never ask you to do something that would hurt you."

"I guess."

"Not good enough."

"I don't know."

"Yes or no," he pressured her.

She paused.

"Look, if you do it, I'll buy you anything that you want in this mall. I'll buy the bloody mall itself."

"Anything?" she asked and Mallory nodded. "Okay."

"Excellent." He grabbed her hand and they raced down the stairs toward the piano. "Play for me."

"Mallory, here?"

"Yes? You're good, aye?"

"Yeah, but in front of all these strangers?"

"I thought it was your passion. That's what you said."

"Yeah, but..."

"Look, my passion is Matthew. If he wanted me to kiss him here, I would. I would shout his name to the high heavens. I would never let anyone get in the way of that."

"Really?"

"Really. Play."

"Okay," she slowly walked up to the piano. "What if I mess up?"

"Start over. I won't mind."

She sat down and ran her fingers down the scales. She paused and looked up at Mallory. "What should I play?"

"Anything."

"What's your favorite?"

"Uh ... Mozart ... any piano concerto."

"Sit with me."

He obliged her and sat next to her with his back turned toward the piano. She started playing soft and slow. After missing a few notes, she stopped. Mallory got up and straddled the bench behind her. He snuggled his hand on her stomach and broadened her posture.

"No one else is here but you and me. Just play for me," he whispered in her ear. She took a deep breath and started playing. Mallory gently tapped her thigh like a metronome. "Close your eyes and breathe, feel the music."

After a while, her notes were flawless. Mallory closed his eyes and inhaled the melody. Her passion flowed through her music. Her body moved as if the notes on the piano possessed it. After she hit the final notes, she fell back into his arms and sighed heavily.

"Damn, you're leaving that for me?"

"Yeah."

Mallory felt sad. "Play another song."

She started playing and Mallory continued his metronome tapping. Once again, her body was possessed and the melody flowed through the air. As his eyes closed, tears fell. This wasn't fair. She was beautiful and talented, and no one should sacrifice his or her talent. When she finished her final notes this time, their intimate conversation was interrupted by loud applause from all levels of the mall. She looked up with a beaming smile. He finally got up and allowed her to take a bow. The crowd finally subsided and she walked toward him. "I've never played in public before."

"I never kissed Matthew in public before," he confessed in laughter.

"You lied."

"No, I said I would, not that I have." He let out a big laugh. "You sound so brilliant."

"Thanks. My gift now, please?"

"Choose?"

"Maybe I'll wait until we get married for you to buy me the mall."

"If we get married, you can buy the mall yourself." Mallory said with a wink. She smiled. "So what do you want?"

"Diamonds."

"Are you old enough for diamonds?"

She laughed grabbing his hand and leading him into an exquisite jewelry store. Before she walked in, she glanced at the diamond crusted charm piano displayed in the window. "That's what I want."

"A charm?"

"Yeah."

"Just a charm?"

"Yeah, I want it to remind me of what I'm leaving."

They strolled into the store and Stacy headed directly for the charm. Mallory walked around looking for a bracelet. When he spotted the perfect platinum diamond charm bracelet, he told another salesperson that he wanted to get the bracelet along with the charm she wanted. He looked around and decided on two other charms — a number three channel set in diamonds and a platinum elephant. He walked back over to Stacy.

"They're going to put it in a box for you."

"Mr. Towneson, will this be on your charge account?" the salesperson asked. Mallory turned to answer discreetly, but he felt Stacy right behind him so he nodded. "Your total will be eighteen, eight-sixty-three." He smiled and nodded again.

"That charm was that expensive?"

"No worries," he walked toward the counter and signed the bill, then instructed the saleswoman to put the charms on the bracelet and put the bracelet in the box. She obliged. Moment, later she re-appeared and handed the box to Stacy. "Now, don't open it until we get back to my office."

They browsed through a few more stores when Mallory realized that it was getting late and it would be best to get her home soon.

"My daddy's car is probably waiting for me at your office."

"You can take your daddy's car or I can take you home."

"My daddy told me not to let you take me home."

"Why?"

"He said that you would take advantage of me."

"I'm taking to your house, not my house. I don't think we're ready for you to come home with me just yet."

"Can I drive?"

"Can you drive?"

"I have my learner's permit," she laughed. Mallory laughed in horror. "Gotcha ... I have a license." She waved it jokingly in his face.

"I wasn't worried," he said as he tossed the keys to her. As the valet brought the car around then opened the door, Mallory walked Stacy over to the driver side and slammed the door. She reopened the driver door and stuck out her tongue, which made Mallory laugh. He finally hopped in the car and turned up the stereo.

"Oh I like this song. Do you know it?"

"This is a provocative song. What are you doing listening to Prince? You're underage."

"I practice my moves listening to Prince songs." She smiled.

"What?"

"Just because I'm a virgin doesn't mean that I'm a good girl."

Mallory was choked up. "Well pull over and I'll sing to you."

"Pull over?"

"This is not a sing and drive song."

She pulled over to the shoulder and put the car in park. Mallory reached over, kissing her neck, hit the button to open the top of the convertible. As he retreated to his side, he grabbed her arms and began serenading her. He pulled her over from the driver side seat. She straddled him and began loosening his tie. He nibbled on her ear and neck and ran his fingers down the spine of her back. Then, he grabbed her hips and started grinding underneath her. She tried to kiss him but he deflected her attempts.

Instead, he licked her lips with his tongue and she melted. Grabbing her hands, he pushed her back then released the lever to let the seat fall back. He lifted his arms above his head while she started unbuttoning his shirt and kissing his chest. He retrieved the gift box in the back seat and handed it her.

She opened it and her eyes beamed. "You got the bracelet too?"

"Yes. You can't have a charm without a bracelet. Regardless, you deserve much more than the bracelet."

She took the bracelet out of the box and Mallory helped her put it on. She kissed him briefly and quickly returned her attention to the bracelet. She was mesmerized by the sparkly diamonds that played against the bright streetlight. She saw the number three charm then laughed, "So you still think I'm three?"

"You're my Three," he tapped a kiss on his lips. He ran his hands through her long wavy hair and pulled her head back. He delivered full body kisses while lowering her body down to his. Although they were passionate, Mallory made sure that his kisses were gentle and not overwhelming. After all, she wasn't Matthew. He caressed her body and felt her excitement rising.

"*Stop Mallory. Stop Mallory!*" He told himself as he realized that her T-shirt was off and landed in the back seat. He attempted to slow her down, pushing her back by grabbing her stomach, but he felt the snap from her bra hit his finger. "*Shit! Stop Mallory! Damn I'm on automatic.*" As he grabbed her hips to pull her away, he found his hands in the mist of her wetness.

Eventually, the screams from Prince in the background caught his attention and he elevated his seat. "Hey we need to go."

"We do?"

"Yes we do! Get up and get back on your side. Now!"

"Why?"

"You won't be a virgin if we continue. I see why your Daddy didn't want you riding with me."

"But I have jeans on."

"Naïve, Three. You don't think I can't get you out of your jeans?" He handed her T-shirt back to her. "I can get the Pope out of his robe."

She giggled as she re-hooked her bra and put her T-shirt back on. She paused for a moment then reached over to kiss him. He knew this was her way of reading him to see if he was angry or upset. He returned a delicate kiss to her lips, and then kissed her nose letting her know everything was fine. She put the car in gear and merged back into traffic. The CD changed and D'Angelo's Crusin' song played.

"Oh I like this song too."

"Maybe I need to put some Sesame Street songs in here. Like C is for couchie ... COOKIE ... cookie, I meant cookie."

She belted out a goofy laugh, which was cute to Mallory.

"Oh damn, girl, let's go home."

She laughed. "Got caught up, huh?"

"You should be so proud."

They finally arrived at her house. She drove up to the driveway slowly. Mallory saw that her father was anxiously standing outside on the porch. "I guess I need to walk you to the door."

"Is that chivalrous?"

"Yes Three," he smiled. He jumped out the car and walked over to the driver side. He opened the door. Just before he helped her out, he snuck a kissed from her as he hit the button to open the trunk. She stepped out of the car with the broadest smile. He collected her bags from the trunk and walked her up to the porch.

As she got close to her daddy, she released Mallory's hand and jumped in her daddy's arms. "Hey, Daddy. Sorry, we didn't go back to the office."

Mallory cringed when her dad flashed his fearful expression.

I like him, Daddy. We went to the mall and he bought me this." She flashed her expensive bracelet quickly. Her daddy barely looked at it because his eyes were fixed on Mallory. "I played Mozart at the mall ... in public, Daddy."

"Good, sweetbee," he said, staring at Mallory.

She jumped out of his arms and grabbed her bags from Mallory, "Mommy?" She ran into the house.

"Mallory?"

"Senator?"

Stacy ran back out, jumped into Mallory's arms, and kissed him. Mallory had mixed feeling of guilt, awkwardness and arousal. He pecked her lips and let her go quickly. "Good night, Mallory."

"Good night, Three." He smiled innocently. She ran back into the house flashing her bracelet to her mom.

"That's a beautiful little girl I have there," The senator said with a quiver in his voice. Mallory knew he was fishing for some truth that she was still the same little girl that left that morning. Although they shared a brief but intense sexual prologue, she was still the same. He thought torturing her father with the vagueness of their events would serve him right for making his daughter leave Juilliard. But he knew that his vagueness would cause more problems for her.

"Yes, she is. She's a beautiful lit-tle girl." He patted the senator on the back then walked off the porch. The senator released a big sigh and waved to Mallory.

When Mallory made it back to the car and turned it on, Prince was blasting loudly. "Till I get your daughter ... I won't leave this town."

When the senator looked back at him, he quickly turned the stereo off. *Now that was a message I wanted to leave him with,* he thought sarcastically.

𝔐

Mallory went back to the office, but he couldn't concentrate on his financial work. Something was missing. He cleared his desk and took out a flipchart pad. He started writing down all of the activities and stunts he had to do for the family business.

"*Marry a virgin, Black Knighthood meetings, major income distribution among four strange divisions, and proselytization before the next lunar eclipse.*"

He circled the proselytization word and marked a big question mark through it. "This doesn't make sense. I'm missing something. This virgin thing is getting to me." He went over the list for hours before giving up and going home.

𝔐

Mallory drove around for hours trying to resolve this dilemma. On his way home, he received a call from Marek. "Towneson."

"Well how was your play date?" Marek laughed.

Mallory heard his other brothers in the background laughing as well. "Interesting," Mallory said strangely.

There was a long silence.

Marek picked up the phone, "MT, what happened?"

"Nothing much, why?"

The speakerphone came back on and Marc was on this time. "What did you do?" Marc asked.

"This and that."

"Mallory, when did you drop her off?" Marek asked.

Mallory briefly glanced at his clock. His clock said 10:45. He dropped her off at 6:30. "Fifteen minutes ago," he lied.

"What did you two do?" Marc screamed.

"A true gentleman doesn't kiss and tell." Mallory tried hard to hold in his laughter.

"Damn it! I knew we should have had a chaperon. Listening to fucking Marc, he said you wouldn't bite because you like getting pumped in the ass."

Mallory laughed. "Marek, you know me baby. If pussy's in the house, I can't resist it. You called it before."

"Damn Mallory! This is fucked up." Marc screamed.

Mallory laughed harder because he could see them sweating. "Look I gotta go and soak in the hot tub, I pulled a groin muscle. You know these young chicks bounce around a lot." He barely hung up the phone before let out a big laugh. He pulled up the driveway and saw lights on in the house. "Oh Matty is home," he rushed through the back door and waltzed in the kitchen to see Matthew slaving over the stove.

"Hey, Emerald."

"Hey love," he kissed him on the shoulder. "I didn't know that you were going to be here. I would have been home sooner."

"I put it on the calendar."

"You don't follow that calendar."

"I guess not. Oh ... you had a message on your machine, but I accidentally erased it." Matthew confessed. "Sorry... but it said Silas is recovering fine but they think he might be blind. Who is Silas?"

"I don't know."

The phone rang. "Who in the hell is that calling this late?"

"My beloved brothers! Don't answer it yet, I have to tell you about my day." Mallory laughed as he sat at the bar.

"Is it a glass of wine story or bottles of wine story?"

"It's a glass of milk story," Mallory laughed. "These motherfuckers set me up with a three-year-old," he laughed. "Apparently, there aren't that many virgins, since they are fucking in elementary schools now."

"Three, Emerald?"

"Okay, she's not three. She's nineteen."

"Damn, aren't you thirty?" Matthew said then quickly turned toward the refrigerator to shield himself from Mallory's harsh response.

"No bitch! Twenty-nine! We turn twenty-nine together this year, and you're much older than I am," he snapped.

"What, by two hours?" Matthew rolled his eyes. "Oh you sound like Marek."

"Anyway, it was wild. You know she called me a faggot in La Madeline's."

"Oh my God, what did you do?"

"I bought her a diamond charm bracelet."

"Damn, I didn't get a diamond bracelet."

"Bitch, I have bought you several damn bracelets and one watch with forty-eight damn diamonds in it that you never wear."

"But it's not a charm bracelet," he kissed him on the cheek and handed him a glass of milk.

"You're an ass." He sat the milk down.

The phone rang again. "Why are they calling?"

"Because they think you're not pumping me in the ass enough and I fucked her."

Matthew's face flashed with horror.

"You know if you ask me that question, I'm going to be hurt, right?"

Matthew tried to retreat his facial expression, but it was too late. Mallory got up from the bar and walked into the kitchen.

"I know better," Matthew said, but it wasn't convincing.

Mallory appeared from the pantry with a handful of Oreos and his milk, "Rubbish." He rolled his eyes as he walked upstairs to his office.

The phone rang again and this time Matthew decided to answer it. "Haulm residence."

"Muthafucka, I have been calling you all night." Marek shouted.

"Why?"

"What's wrong with Mallory?"

"I don't know... what's wrong with him?"

"Are you not fucking him? Oh, that's nasty. You make sure that you two do that nasty-mc-nasty shit you two do. He doesn't need to be fucking that girl until the wedding day."

"Well maybe you should have thought of that before setting him up on a play date. Maybe you should have told him the wedding date and had him show up."

"Look punk ..."

"No you look muthafucka! I don't control Emerald. He makes his own decisions. If you weren't so busy trying to control his life, you would see that he generally does the right thing. The more you try to control him the more he acts out."

"So you don't think?"

"No, I don't think he fucked her. In fact, I know that he didn't. He wouldn't do that to me!" he paused because he wanted Mallory to hear his defense but Mallory wasn't around. "Get off my fucking phone!" He slammed the phone down.

Mallory sat at his desk swirling around in his chair. He picked up his universal remote, selected his office for the room and turned on Mozart. He closed his eyes and reminisced about Stacy's performance.

Matthew knocked on the door but there was no answer. He walked into hear Mozart blasting and Mallory's eye closed.

"Emerald, I'm sorry."

Mallory opened his eyes but didn't look in his direction.

"I know better. Look, baby let's go to bed."

Mallory rolled his eyes down in disgust. "I don't feel like getting pumped tonight."

"Stop saying that. That's so vulgar. I wasn't suggesting sex; it's midnight. Anyway, sex doesn't fix everything."

"No it doesn't. Especially when I'm faithful and nobody believes me."

"Emerald, I believe you."

"And then you're going to lie to me to my face? Just go to bed."

"EM ..." Matthew caught the music. "Mozart?"

"It calms me."

"Since when?"

"Since now!"

Matthew laughed nervously, "I learn something new about you everyday."

"... Like I can be faithful. Just go to bed. I'll be there in a minute." Mallory closed his eyes and resumed listening. When his monitor flashed a message, he opened his eyes and glanced at his screen. He clicked on the screen and it was a message from Stacy.

Hey Mallory.

Thank you for a wonderful time. I hope I wasn't too much of a brat. I'm psyched about my bracelet. It's so cute. Mommy's hating. Daddy thinks it's too expensive for a girl my age. They're arguing about it now. I wanted to invite you to my recital in Houston. I'm playing with the Houston Symphony. I'm so excited. I hope you can come. I might need you to keep my time. I appreciate my private song in the car. You have a good night. Thank you.

Signed, Three."

Before Mallory thought, he clicked reply.

You're welcome. Yes, you were a little brat. But I guess that I was a grumpy old man. That bracelet looked beautiful on you. Let your mom wear it sometime. It's not too expensive for you if you're going to be my wife. Furthermore, that's not the last expensive gift you'll get from me.... Get use to it. I'll give you the world if you like ... or at least a mall. Give me the date of your recital and I'll be there. I'll even sit with you if you need it. You play so beautifully. I can just hear you now. Good night, my love.

Signed, Caught up."

CHAPTER TEN

After a long day, Mallory strolled into the house to find it in shambles. Clothes were scattered on the couch and chaise lounge, and luggage was half-packed. Matthew was leaving again. He bowed his head as he made his way through the maze of scattered clothes to Matthew's bedroom.

Not knowing that Mallory was standing in the doorway, Matthew was singing gospel full blast. Mallory became infuriated with each note Matthew sang. Matthew finally looked down and saw Mallory sitting ominously quiet. He pulled the earpieces out and sat next to him on the bed.

"You can't control my personal CD collection."

Mallory looked down.

"Do you want to listen to it? You'll like it."

Mallory got up and walked out without speaking.

Matthew followed him into the kitchen. "I didn't feel like cooking ..."

Mallory managed to muster up concern. "What do you feel like eating?"

"Nothing."

"Are you fasting now?" Mallory asked coldly, to which Matthew responded by turning his back and sitting at the bar. Mallory pulled out a bottle of cold wine from the mini wine cellar and poured a glass. He looked at Matthew and started to ask if he wanted one, but decided not to. "Don't you think you need nourishment if you're traveling?"

"I'll eat at sundown."

"Sundown is it?" Mallory gulped down the glass of wine and loosened his tie, "I know this is falling on deaf ears, but I don't want you to go."

"I understand your concern, but this is important to me."

"Am I important to you?" He poured another glass of wine.

Matthew turned to face Mallory and said sincerely, "Yes, Emerald. But if I don't find these answers, I'll go crazy. Can you love a crazy man?"

"I love you! I don't care how you are."

"This is my —"

"PLEASE DON'T SAY THIS IS MY LAST TRIP!" he snapped. "Hearing those bloody words burns me." He wanted to grab Matthew and hug him tightly, but he decided to keep his distance. He downed another glass of wine. "So you're fasting and praying tonight and maybe I'll get a handshake in the morning before you go?"

"Emerald, you know that I've never left you with a handshake."

"You've been home for three weeks and you haven't touched me once. This last time, you resorted to sleeping in separate beds. It seems that every time you come back from these trips, you want me less and less." He poured another glass of wine. "Do you not want us?"

"What does it matter? You're getting married."

"That's what this is about? My paper marriage? My charade of a marriage. Nobody believes that this marriage is real. It's a farce."

"If it's so much of a farce, why did you get a wedding present today?" Matthew pointed to the oversized brown paper wrapping in the living room.

"Huh?" Mallory walked toward it, viewing the mailing label.

"Who is Elektra?"

Mallory knew the question was rhetorical. "She's an artist." He said as he downed another glass.

"Local artist?" Matthew knew Elektra or Brielle, but Mallory didn't want to give him any ammunition for an argument so he decided to retreat.

"Ok, Matty, have it your way."

"Open it."

"You open it. I need to take a shower." Mallory walked off.

Matthew grabbed the empty bottle of wine and threw it at the painting, tearing the brown paper a little. Through the new hole peered a pair of sharp, piercing painted eyes that looked very familiar. He walked toward the painting and began removing the brown paper, giving way to a black and gray statue of a man with piercing eyes, dressed in black, walking out of ash and black smoke. He saw the same painting in the caves.

Strange. He must have told someone about the trip, he thought.

Scribbled across the bottom was *Death cometh alive.* The man stood tall and very strong, and was carrying a double-edged sword. His pale face was painted with such anger and strength that it sent shivers down Matthew's spine. As he looked toward the man's feet, he saw bodies of children and adults bowing down to him and dying. He looked at the image deeper. Behind that man was another man dressed in celestial white kneeling over in pain with a sword protruding out of his body and his wings covered in blood.

As Matthew gazed closer at the image, the wings flapped and the head rose up then screamed, "I need you to be strong."

Matthew jumped and quickly walked away into the kitchen. He flashed a fake smile when he heard Mallory come back into the room. "You're right, I need to eat."

"It's not sundown, yet." Mallory said sarcastically. He opened another wine bottle and poured another glass.

"But you said I needed nourishment."

"Okay, what do you want?"

"Whatever you're cooking?"

"I was thinking take-out?"

"We've never had take-out before," Matthew chuckled.

"I have never been *this* angry with you before."

"Never mind," he huffed.

"Okay," Mallory felt that old feeling of guilt welling up in his stomach. "I'll cook for you. What do you want?"

"Nothing."

"Look Matthew. I'm really trying to be patient here. I'm trying to be understanding. I'm trying to be here for you, but you're fucking-testing my got damn patience here!" Mallory slammed the wine bottle on the bar, shattering it to pieces.

Matthew made no eye contact with him. "Like I said, I want nothing." Matthew walked away coldly.

Frustrated, Mallory banged his head down on the granite bar.

Peter ran out to see the commotion. "Are you okay, sir?"

"I really need to take that shower."

It was sundown and Matthew stood in the doorway of Mallory's bedroom watching him in the bed. He finally crawled into bed, laying on Mallory, kissing and tonguing his body.

Mallory didn't respond. He finally reached his face and traced his ear gently. Still, there was no response.

"Emerald?"

"WHAT?"

"Baby, I want you. It's our last night."

"I know."

"You know how we celebrate our last night together."

"I don't want to do it."

Matthew sat up abruptly. "Are you sick? There has never been a time you never wanted to fuck me. Not even the time I played gospel on your damn precious sound system."

"Make sure you take that shit out of my system."

"Fine, I will. But what's really wrong?"

Mallory sat up and faced him. "Didn't I tell you that I was a fucking jealous God? Did you think that was a bloody joke? Didn't I say that I don't want any motherfucker above me?"

"Emerald, stop. Come on. I want you."

"Fuck Him. Have Him satisfy you. He's your all in all. He's your Savior. Let His bitch ass work it out."

"Emerald, stop this. I don't want to spend our last night like this."

"I don't care how you want to spend it...I'm not in the mood."

"You're always in the mood." He gave him a friendly pinch on the cheek. "That's just who you are. When you're dead and buried, you'll still be in the mood."

"Well, I'm not in the mood for you!" Mallory slapped Matthew's hand away and turned over covering his head.

"Fine," Matthew jumped out of the bed and walked out.

"Where are you going?"

"Why do you care? You're an unforgiving God and I have no room for that." Matthew slammed the door. He walked into the kitchen and poured himself a tall glass of wine then he strolled toward the life-size painting and studied it intimately. He noticed that the painting resembled Mallory.

When he went to touch it, the man in the painting drew his sword. Matthew fell back on the floor, dropping the glass of wine. The man jumped out of the painting with one thunderous stomp, swinging his sword high above his head. As he lunged after Matthew, he struck the wall shattering a crystal vase. Matthew quickly scooted back trying to get away. He swung again and barely missed Matthew, striking the chaise lounge. Matthew tried to get up again, but his socks gave him no friction against the freshly buffed hardwood floor. The man swung again, striking the hardwood floor just barely missing Matthew. He finally got up and ran back toward the bedroom. Just then, Mallory walked out of the bedroom and they collided, falling to the floor.

"What the bloody hell are you doing?" Mallory shouted.

"Get up, Emerald! That fucking thing is after me?"

"The got damn cloud again?"

"No!" Matthew scrambled to get up and turned toward the painting but the man was back in it. He looked over at the wall and chaise lounge but didn't see any damage to the room. He sat back on the floor in shock.

"What it is?"

"Nothing. I guess the painting scared me."

Mallory started laughing. "You're scared of acrylic paint, now?"

"Piss off. I'm horny. I scare easily when I'm horny."

Mallory finally got up and walked toward the painting. "It's just acrylic paint." Mallory went to touch the painting and the man's hand touched his. He moved his hand up and then down and the man's hand followed every movement. Mallory glided his fingertips down the sword and cut his finger. "Shit."

"What? You're still teasing me. I don't like that painting, Emerald. I'm not sleeping with that painting in the house."

"Okay, let's take it to the garage." He nursed his finger in his mouth.

Really? That was too easy, Matthew thought. Matthew quickly walked over to the painting and grabbed one side before Mallory could change his mind.

Mallory grabbed the other side of the painting. As he guided Matthew through the living room, Mallory walked on the damaged hardwood floor and caught a splinter. "Shit!"

"What's wrong?" Matthew dropped his side of the painting.

"What the fuck happened to my hardwood floor?" Mallory saw a big gouge in the floor. Matthew's mouth flew open as he looked at the floor. Although he was scared, he felt better because the gouge was proof he wasn't losing his mind and that something was after him, but he wasn't going to tell Mallory.

"I don't know. You need help with your foot?"

"No, I can get it out." Mallory managed to take the splinter out of his foot.

They grabbed the painting again and continued to move it out. When they finally reached the garage, Mallory went to the side door and opened the automatic doors. Matthew looked down at the painting again and the hand of the man was reaching for him. He dropped the painting quickly and it landed backside up. The door finally opened and Mallory saw the painting lying on the ground. "Look bitch, be careful! That's my fucking wedding present."

"It was heavy." Matthew snapped back. "Damn! You sound like Marek."

"Why don't you just admit that you don't want me to get married?"

"I admit it. I don't want you to get married," Matthew paused. "That doesn't mean that I don't love you or I don't want to be with you. You're punishing me."

Mallory shrugged off his explanation as he grabbed the painting forcefully. Matthew; however, cautiously picked it up from his side. They placed it in a room where household tools were kept.

"Have you ever been in this room? This doesn't look like you."

"It's my damn house."

They stepped back and noticed that the painting looked unusually angry.

"You know what? Let's turn it around. I don't want to scare Harold when comes down here. This is his room."

Matthew finally heard a snicker as he helped Mallory turn the painting. As they left the garage, Matthew gently grabbed Mallory's face and kissed him softly, but Mallory broke the kiss.

"You're still mad?"

"Yes. You keep going back to Jerusalem and I keep having to save you. Every time you come back, something crazy weird is after you. And you won't even touch me. But on the last night, you want to fuck like crazy? It's like I have to reset you. These trips are getting to me."

"I said this was my last trip."

"How many times have you told me that? Remember when you almost died of heat stroke, or the first of the three times the cave collapsed and I didn't hear from you for two months. Or how about that time you refused to take the jet and if I didn't cancel your fucking reservations, you would have died in that plane crash?"

"Emerald, I'm at the end."

"Really? What are you looking for?"

"You have not been listening to me all these years?"

"Yes, I've been listening all these years but all I'm hearing is that you don't know if God exists."

"He does exist!"

"YES HE DOES! And his name is Mallory Towneson Haulm, remember?" Mallory tugged at his pendant.

Matthew dipped his eyes and said, "I don't want to fight with you tonight."

"And I don't want to compete with HIM ever!"

Matthew finally retreated and walked back into the house. Mallory followed, but paused when Matthew went to his bedroom.

Mallory was baffled. "Where are you going now?"

"If my God can't please me, I don't need to be in his presence." Matthew said arrogantly.

It took everything that Mallory had not to grab Matthew and strangle him. "So let it be written, you won't get fucked tonight."

"Let it be so." Without another word, Matthew walked in his bedroom and slammed the door.

Mallory was outdone. He sat at the bar and slumped over. He didn't want to fight with Matthew; however, his patience was quickly disappearing. He needed to make a stand if Matthew was going to ever take him seriously. It had been three years since Matthew began searching for answers to a truth that Mallory couldn't comprehend. He walked up to Matthew's door and wanted to knock on it, but stopped. He stood there for a long time contemplating what he was going to say. After awhile, he decided that he was going to keep his stance in silence, so he returned to his room.

"He'll come for me. I'll give in then." As he waited, he fell fast asleep.

The next morning, Matthew made the final preparations for his last trip to Jerusalem. He truly believed that he was at the end of his search. He also knew that Mallory was at the end of his patience rope. He couldn't put his finger on it, but he knew Mallory's marriage to Stacy wasn't right. With the other information that Mallory told him about joining the family business, the signs were so apparent, but Matthew couldn't see it. He couldn't get Mallory to see it either, so he made Mallory believe the marriage would hinder their relationship.

He stepped into the master bedroom and found Mallory still sleeping. He stood at the edge of the bed. "Emerald turn over," no response. He climbed into bed and nudged him. "Emerald turn over."

"What?" He fussed.

"Turn over, baby," he begged.

Mallory grudgingly turned over but didn't open his eyes.

Matthew pulled the bottom of the sheets over him and climbed partially on Mallory. "What are you doing?"

Matthew tugged at his pajamas. Soon his question was answered. Mallory could feel Matthew's warm tongue circle his tip, and then envelop his gulf of heat.

"Don't do that! Oh shit ... that feels so good." Mallory bit his lower lip. "Oh shit, Matty. Stop Mat ... oh shit." Mallory grabbed the mattress and squeezed it hard with each suction. "Oh fuck!" Mallory screamed as he came.

Matthew rushed up and gave him a hard open mouth kiss. A few seconds later, he stopped and Mallory popped out his mouth guard.

"Now I got fucking sperm on my guard."

"Emerald, get up."

"Why?"

"I'm leaving."

"I know."

"You're not going to walk me out?"

"No."

"Why?"

"You're leaving me."

"Emerald ..."

"No! Get off me," he shrugged.

"Emerald, you know you're going to regret not walking me out."

"I regret it now. That doesn't mean I'm going to get up."

"Emerald, this is my last trip."

"RUBBISH!"

"Emerald, I'm serious. I promise you...this time if I don't find anything, I'll quit."

"You keep saying that. Get off me or you're going be late for your little commercial flight."

"Emerald, you know I can't take the jet. You'll convince me to stay longer, and I would miss the last discovery."

"Well then get the fuck up!" he shouted.

"I don't want you to be angry."

"You can't have it both ways, Matty. Either you cancel your trip, not fucking delay it but cancel the trip now, or suffer my wrath ... I mean the consequence. Just listening to your God shit has fucked up my vocabulary."

"It hasn't disturbed your obscenities, mini Marek."

"What do you want from me?"

"Your support."

"I have supported you for three fucking years. When have you supported me?"

"Don't start this again."

"Why not? I'm getting married in two days, and you won't be there."

"I told you I can't be there."

"Fine, get the fuck up!" Mallory managed to lift Matthew's body and flip him over. He was on top this time. "You know what, I changed my bloody mind. You're going no fucking where. You're going to miss your got damn commercial flight and stay here with me. You wanna fuck now?"

"Emerald." Matthew said calmly. Mallory placed all his dead weight on Matthew. "You can't do this, EM." Matthew waited a few moments and said, "Uh, I can taste your sperm swimming in my mouth."

Mallory jumped up. "You little bitch." He jumped out of bed, grabbed his guard and ran to the master bath.

Matthew stayed in bed laughing. "You and strange tastes. Would you like for me to bring you a shot of Absolut?" He mimicked Peter's voice then laughed harder. He finally got up and met Mallory in the bathroom, who just finished brushing his teeth and gargling. Mallory was rinsing out his guard when he saw Matthew in the mirror. Rolling his eyes, he placed the guard back in his mouth. He knew Matthew hated that guard when they kissed. "So now you're up ... walk me out."

"I said NO!" Mallory shouted as he pushed passed Matthew and jumped back in bed, covering his head.

"You're being a little bitch today."

"Isn't it my month?"

"You better be careful, I might bring back some tampons." Matthew sat on the side of the bed and attempted to remove the covers. "Emerald."

"Don't touch me."

"I told you even if I didn't have this trip, I wouldn't go to that wedding."

Mallory sat up. "You know I'm getting married and it would be great, just this once, to have my only best mate there by my side."

"Emerald, I can't be at that wedding. It doesn't feel right. How do you think it makes me feel to hear her saying vows to you that I should be saying?"

"It's a paper marriage."

"It's a sacred ceremony."

"I still need you there."

"I can't."

"Fine, walk your damn self out." Mallory laid back down and covered his head.

Matthew closed his eyes. He didn't know where the words were coming from but he knew he needed to say them. "Emerald, I was thinking ... maybe you need to consummate the marriage."

Mallory removed the covers and sat up again. "I can't believe you. Why would you say that to me?"

"I don't know ... but it just seems like the right thing to say."

"What does the phrase 'paper marriage' mean to you?"

"It means you're not legally mine. You belong to her."

"She has my name, nothing else. You have my heart, remember?" Matthew looked away but Mallory took his chin and held it up. He looked deeply into Matthew's eyes. "I told you that it was a marriage on paper only and that I just needed some time to get on the board and figure out how to get out of it." Matthew looked away again. "Something else is bothering you, isn't it? It's that God shit."

"Stop saying God shit."

"Every time you go on one of these fucking trips, more distance grows between us. Sometimes, I don't know what's worse, you leaving or you coming home. I'm not competing with Him, Matthew!"

"This is my last trip. After this and your wedding...let's talk about everything."

"No, let's talk about this now."

"I can't. I gotta go."

"So I'm not important to you?"

"Yes, you're very important to me, baby."

"But not important enough to stay?"

Matthew couldn't respond. He kissed Mallory on the forehead and said, "I love you, Emerald."

For the first time since they had been together, Mallory didn't respond. Matthew turned away and walked out of the room quietly, closing the door. Mallory took off his ring and threw it across the room then laid back down.

Matthew passed the kitchen to find Peter waiting for him. Matthew frowned when he saw Peter with a glowing aura around him. "Peter, you're glowing."

"You see my true presence?"

"True presence?"

Peter grabbed Matthew and rushed him out of the house. "Quick, before he puts another spell on you."

"What are you talking about?"

"Mallory, here," He shoved files in Matthew's arms. "These are his medical records. Find out the truth about Mallory. Quick! Leave before he comes out."

Matthew was rushed into the car and was whisked away. Peter looked back to find that Mallory wasn't standing there. He walked back into the house and noticed that the bedroom door was still closed. "This is strange. He always comes for Matthew." He jiggled the doorknob to find that the door was locked. He looked down and saw black smoke flowing from underneath the door.

"Master Mallory, are you okay?" Peter asked nervously.

"I'm fine," he said with an ominous undertone.

Peter stepped back in fear. "Oh my God."

The door flung open and Mallory appeared out of the dark room and shouted, "Never call His name in my house. You know better."

CHAPTER ELEVEN

When Matthew's plane finally landed in Jerusalem, he was the last person to exit. As he walked slowly to the baggage claim and stood in the immigration line, he could feel the distance growing between him and Mallory. He couldn't explain it, but the feelings of love and devotion were turning into hatred and anger. This change saddened him. He exited the airport and found his car. The driver grabbed his things and he settled in, lying back in the seat. The voices of Peter and the professors began ringing in his head.

Stop protecting him. Piercing eyes. Learn the truth. Evil temper, anger, coldness. You're blinded. Skin of ice.

When Matthew attempted to rub the frustration off his face, his fingertips grazed his lips. He vaguely remembered Mallory feeling like a Popsicle. His kisses were ice cold and his body was freezing. Matthew closed his eyes, recalling the frost that escaped Mallory's breath when he spoke. His eyes were changing from green to blue before him.

"It can't be," he said, but the voices kept shouting.

Stop protecting him. Piercing eyes. Learn the truth"

Matthew tried again to shake the thoughts and voices out of his head. "I need to call him." He mentally shut down the wrestling in his head as the car turned into the exploration site. When he stepped out of the car, the professors rushed toward him.

"Are you okay, sir?"

"Why?" he frowned.

"You have aged," one professor said.

Matthew looked at his hands and they were winkled and dry.

"We understand what happened. Come into the cave and we'll explain to you." They rushed him deep inside the cave. Once they reached the part of the cave where the monks were, they shoved him up against the wall and forced him down. They attempted to take the ring from his finger.

"What are you doing? No! Emerald gave me that! Give it back." Matthew fought back hard, but he was outnumbered. One professor managed to take the ring off then pushed him down on the holy ground. Matthew lay on the ground for the longest time. "Emerald! Explain NOW!"

"He's not Emerald. You have been poisoned."

Just then, a great white cloud appeared, filling every inch of the cave. The cloud grew past the walls and consumed everything in sight, which scared Matthew. The professors and monks disappeared in the cloud.

"You're my nightmare."

"No, son. I AM your Father," The commanding voice stated.

"What?"

"You were lost. I feared I was going to lose you for good."

"What are you? Who are you?"

"You know who I am, son. I am the Great I AM."

Matthew squeezed his temples, trying to stop the pain from rushing through his head. His hands began aching and he felt feverishly hot. He tried focusing on the great cloud, but he couldn't. He finally opened his eyes and looked up beyond the ceiling.

"Son, don't fight it. You were sent on a quest and you got lost. I tried to let you find your way back."

"Quest?" He thought hard, *My assignment?*

"Do you know your assignment?"

"I was supposed to kill The Final."

"Do you know the final?"

"No," he frowned and shook his head.

"Open your mind's eye, son."

Matthew squeezed his eyes closed, but his head really began aching and he found it hard to breathe. Memories of Mallory in college flashed in his mind. Matthew watched him from a distance. He remembered that he was determined to get close to him to kill him. He thought that would be easier than a battle.

"Son, what were the warnings about The Final?"

"Never look in his eyes. Never touch him. Never kill him in the cold. Find a higher ground. One swift cut to the neck." He dropped his head, "I failed, Father. I failed."

"It's not too late."

"What will you have me do, Father?"

"Continue your path. You have one more time before he converts. Remember, the warnings."

"Yes, Father."

The cloud disappeared and the professors and monks gathered around him. "Do you think you can destroy him? Do you know how to destroy him?"

"Yes, it's in the drawings." Matthew finally stood up and walked toward the cave walls where the drawings of a great battle were. He glanced over to the end and saw the black hole. "What happened?"

"He destroyed it. He knows the story and he destroyed it with his hand."

"He doesn't know the story. I would be dead if he knew the story." Matthew thought back to that day. Mallory didn't appear to be evil, mean or strong; rather he was scared and helpless. Matthew remembered helping him up from the ground and Mallory feverishly rubbing his hand after the cave collapsed. "He touched the wall ... to brace himself. He doesn't know the story. He didn't know what he was looking at. He doesn't believe any of this." Matthew laughed hysterically. After a while, his laughter turned into pained tears.

"Sir, are you okay?"

Matthew fell to his knees, laughing as he began to sob. "He doesn't know. He thinks he's some pompous ass atheist who is in love with an angel. Oh my God! He doesn't know. I need to call him."

"He has great power over you. You must destroy this." The professor handed the ring back to Matthew and he looked at it closely.

"This is not the source of his power. The source is the ring I gave him. My Father's ring." He planted his head between his knees and thought back to when he first gave Mallory the ring, the day after Mallory buried his daughter.

Matthew went over to Mallory's apartment to kill him that day. He found Mallory in a corner, crying with a bottle of sleeping pills and a full bottle of gin. He walked up to him with his sword firmly in his hands. He aimed for his neck, but when Mallory looked up, their eyes lock. Matthew's heart filled up with Mallory's pain and despair. He dropped his sword and fell at Mallory's feet. He wanted to comfort him. He managed to get the pills from Mallory and carried him to the shower. He held him tight as Mallory cursed, screamed and cried.

At some point, they both fell asleep. He recalled waking up to find Mallory turning off the shower and handing him a towel. He looked into Mallory's eyes and the colors changed from blue to green. He followed Mallory to the bedroom, where Mallory handed him a pair of sweats. He took Matthew's wet clothes and disappeared in the other room. Matthew looked around the room and saw pictures of baby Rachael and a painted picture of a woman who resembled Mallory. When Mallory appeared back into the room, their eyes were lost in each other and their expressions were of confusion.

He couldn't recall who initiated it, but that night they shared an innocent kiss. In looking back now, it wasn't so innocent. From that day forth, Matthew craved Mallory's touch but he couldn't resolve the craving. He ached for his presence and attention. He remembered that he stopped trying to resolve it once Mallory told him that he loved him.

"I'm the reason he hasn't converted. I deflected him from his path." He went to place the ring back on his finger and the ground shook violently; everyone fell to the ground. The ring flew out of his hand and landed on holy ground. He started crawling toward the holy ground to retrieve the ring but the ground opened up and swallowed up the ring.

CHAPTER TWELVE

After a restless night, Mallory finally arrived at the chapel. It was his wedding day. He felt unusually cold and strangely vulnerable. He couldn't catch his breath and his body shook uncontrollably. As he leaned against the doors of the church, he looked up and a crucifix of Jesus Christ was hanging in front of him.

"Why couldn't this be at a hotel?"

He closed his eyes and managed to walk past the crucifix, regaining a little strength with each step. He started looking for the groom's room but ducked in a corner when he heard Malcolm's voice. Malcolm and Uncle Mal were in a heated debate and didn't notice Mallory hiding. As they turned the corner, Mallory released a sigh and continued his journey. He reached the room and heard another intense argument on the other side.

"Marc, let me handle Mallory," Marek pleaded. "He goes off every time you two are together. He'd go left just because you suggested right. And you don't know how to suggest, you order."

"Fuck that little faggot. He'll get married today or he'll die."

"Marc, you don't mean that. We need him. Just let me handle him. Please?"

"Okay! But the second it gets out of control ..."

Mallory took a deep breath and entered the room, slamming the door behind him. With his eyes closed, he leaned on the door to regain more strength. He finally opened his eyes and found Marc and Marek impatiently waiting for him.

"What do you want, Marc?" he shouted.

Marc stood up in a confrontation stance, but Marek stepped in front of him. "He was just trying to see ... uh ... what kind of bottled water you wanted. You need to stay hydrated for the big day." Marek smiled nervously.

"Penta thanks," Mallory said as he dropped his bags on the ground.

Marc walked out of the room without a response but kept a glaring eye on Mallory.

"Penta? I thought you would say Evian or Deja Blue."

"He'll never find Penta in Austin. Besides, I knew you were lying. I'm just helping you out." He shuffled to the couch and flopped down.

"Thanks, bro. You wanna help me out, marry this girl."

"I'm here, aren't I?"

"Yeah, but I feel that something's gonna go wrong."

"Well the last time you supervised me, we had fun and I did what I was supposed to do."

"Right right. Okay, I'm trippin'. Can I get you anything?"

"What I want is in Jerusalem."

"Matthew?" He frowned.

"I miss him so much."

"I can tell. That's shitty that he wouldn't come to your wedding. He could have been here as your brother or best man. He was your best man," Marek joked and felt relieved when Mallory chuckled.

"I love him so much."

"Why?"

"You're not going to understand."

"Make me."

"He has this energy about him. Every time he's around, I want to touch him and hold him. And it's not about the sex, but that's the only way I can express my craving. I literally crave him. And when he's not around, I can't see, I can't breathe or think. I feel like I'm dying."

"That shit is unhealthy," Marek said under his breath.

"I think something is wrong, Marek."

"Yeah there is," Marek was distracted in thought. "Oh what were you talking about?"

"I don't think he loves me anymore."

"What? Not love you? That nasty shit that you two do?" He grimaced then tried to portray a concerned face. "He's probably just mad because you're getting married. Maybe he thinks you might be switching teams again."

"No, that's not it. He has been doing this God shit, and I think he thinks that I'm a bad person." Mallory shifted from the couch to his knees. "Do you ever get the feeling that something is right in front of you but you can't see it?"

"Nope."

"You know. You're supposed to do or be something but you have no clue?"

"Nope. What the fuck are you talking about?"

Mallory huffed. "He has been studying Revelations and traveling to find the fourth horseman, death."

"Now that's the dumbest shit I have ever heard. He's been looking for what he has been fucking all these years. Now that's some stupid shit."

"What?" Mallory's voice cracked and his face went pale.

Marek looked over and saw Mallory turn as white as a sheet. "Tell me you knew?" He grabbed Mallory's shoulder to stop him from falling. "Shit, I was right! Look, I wanted to say something a long time ago, but Marc thought you were jerking us around. You're the fourth horseman, Death!" Marek quickly ran to the door and locked it. He quickly walked back to Mallory and sat beside him. "I knew you didn't know when you were questioning our financials. And you had a big blank look on your face every time we attended Black Knighthood meetings."

"I'm what?" Mallory was horror-stricken.

"The fourth horseman, Death. Remember Uncle M-Lee, his wife. Those cold feelings you get. The death chant you sing that freaks us out every time you sing it? Death. You are Death!"

"Wait a minute. The cold chills...which explains the feelings at the hospital?" Mallory grabbed his hair and attempted to pull it out of his head. "I'm who?"

"DEATH! You complete us. It ends with you."

"That makes you ..."

"War. I fucking fight all the time. Marines! "

"And Marlon ..."

"You should guess Marlon."

"Famine. He eats all the time."

"Yep, and Marc is the first. But the first doesn't make him a leader. He's just a fucking pest."

"Pestilence."

"Shit, I thought it was Plague."

"It can be both, or disease." Mallory's face grew paler as he started breathing erratically. "I can't believe this ..."

"Are you okay?"

"No, I don't need this on my wedding day, Marek. I really don't need this." Mallory threw his face in his hands and tears started falling from his eyes.

"Man, you'll be alright." Marek patted him on the back. "I wonder why Matthew is looking for the fourth horseman."

Mallory whispered, "He's looking for The Final."

"Oh shit! That's a ruthless muthafucka. We don't want him either."

Mallory looked up with tear-filled eyes.

"That mean son-of-a-bitch will kill everything. Shit I'm in my prime. I'm thinking about World War four, five and fucking six. If he comes tomorrow we're all gone."

Mallory slammed his face in his hands.

"Look, since you know the truth, you need to know the whole truth."

"I can't take anymore." More tears fell from Mallory's eyes.

"Okay, well let me leave you with this. She needs to be fucked before midnight. And some kinda fucking way, you need to suck her blood."

"So I'm a fucking vampire, now?"

"No! It's just a ritual to combine your life forces. We feed on their ability to procreate."

"That's why we can't divorce them?"

"That's right. Then we replace them when they die if we want to live longer lives. Somebody needs to talk with that got damn pink bunny to create a horseman battery."

"She has to be a virgin because of a pure connection?" Words fell out of Mallory's mouth but he couldn't believe what he was saying.

"Ding! Ding! Ding! Give that man a fucking prize. Can't put a used battery in a horseman. It is said that first loves last the longest. That's why you never forget your first time. We thought you were just sabotaging your proselytization. Shit, you were fucking everything you saw."

"You should have just told me."

"I wanted to! But Marc ..."

"Hey, do me a favor?"

"What?"

"Keep him away from me?"

"Sure man. Anything else?"

Mallory asked, "If I need to talk to you?"

"Anytime! There's more to it than just what I told you. But I'm gonna let you get married first. Shit to me, that's the hardest part." Marek walked out of the room.

Mallory stood up and started undressing. Cold sharp pains exploded through his body. He tried bracing himself but he fell over, knocking down the table and chairs. spilling water that was in the vase. The room started spinning and closing in on him. Mallory fell to the floor and start seizing and jerking.

Marek returned to the room and saw that Mallory was suffering an attack. "Oh shit! Mallory, what's wrong?"

Mallory couldn't speak. The room grew black and cold. More sharp pains were splitting his joints in two.

Marc came in the room and noticed Mallory's condition. "OH DAMN, I'll get Dad." He ran out and came back with Malcolm and Uncle Mal.

"Get him on the couch." Uncle Mal asked. "What happened?"

"It looks like a panic attack?" Marek said.

"This is no panic attack. He's dueling himself and won't accept his other side," Malcolm sat Mallory up and overlapped him. "It's no big deal. I've been through this before. Get out, I'll handle this."

The boys started to walk out but paused when they heard Malcolm slap him.

"Should we leave him?" Marek asked.

"GET OUT!" Malcolm shouted as he repeatedly slammed Mallory's head against the wooden edge of the couch.

Marc walked out but Marek couldn't move. He couldn't protect Mallory when he was little, so he felt this was the only time that he was able to protect him. "Dad, don't hurt him please."

Malcolm stood up, grabbed Mallory and threw him up against the wall. Mallory slid down the wall. Malcolm grabbed him again and slapped him across the face.

Marek ran over to them, pulling Malcolm back, and shielding Mallory. "No, Dad, please."

Malcolm grabbed both of them and threw them on the floor. Marek turned his body toward Mallory, shielding him again. Malcolm towered over them, grabbing Mallory's shoulders. "Stop fighting. Accept it or die."

Mallory managed to control his seizures long enough to answer Malcolm.

Malcolm slammed his head on the floor and walked out. Marek lay still over Mallory's cold body. He was still shivering and seizing. Marek finally rose up and carefully helped Mallory back on the couch.

"I'm so sorry for that." Marek said.

Mallory nodded his head while Marek wiped the blood from his mouth and tears from his eyes.

"Can I get you anything?"

Mallory shook his head no. He finally got up and walked over to the sink. He felt the seizures creeping up again but he tried to control them.

"Hey, I think I got some rum in the car. I don't think it's gonna help but …"

Mallory shook his head aimlessly. As Marek walked out, Melody snuck in, looking for Mallory. He painted the weakest smile and gave her a hardy hug.

"I heard that you had a panic attack, sweetie."

He nodded his head.

"Well, you know I almost had a heart attack when I opened your wedding invitation."

His painted smile began to melt with each tear that fell.

"Oh little boy, you're going to be fine." She grabbed his head and placed it between her oversized breasts. She rocked him for a long while.

Marek walked back in the room and noticed that Mallory found comfort, which relieved him a bit. He locked the door and went in search of a couple of glasses.

Mallory lay back on the couch. Melody went into her clutch and pulled out a small-jeweled pillbox. "I'm not supposed to do this. Take one of these." She handed him a nice size pill. "I'm going to leave so you can get dressed." She rose up but Mallory grabbed her hand, pulling her back. "Now, I know that you don't want me to dress you?" She tried hard to lighten the mood but he didn't respond with his usual sexual comments. She leaned over him and kissed his forehead. "It's okay, baby. I'll pray for you. Put it in the Lord's hands. He will work it all out for you."

Those words were the very words that Mallory didn't want to hear. They stirred up feelings of anger he had seeded for Matthew; but somehow this anger warmed him and calmed him down. His expression changed and he regained his composure. He returned the kiss on her cheek and flashed a half-hearted grin. She walked out just when Marek returned with two plastic cups. Mallory threw the pill in his mouth, grabbed the bottle from Marek, and chugged it down.

"Damn! Be careful."

Mallory walked away without saying a word. He gathered his tuxedo and started dressing. Marek noticed that Mallory's spirit was gone and he was going through the motions like a drone. Marek begged Marc to let him handle this, but this was going badly. He felt that he owed Mallory something, but he did not know what. There was a knock on the door.

"What the fuck do you want?" Marek shouted.

"It's me, Marc. Is he ready?"

"Wait, bitch. Check on the bride. Them bitches are always late."

Mallory finalized his primping and chugged another drink. Marek walked up to him and caught a glance of Mallory's eyes changing colors. He wanted to look closer but Mallory lowered his head to rinse his mouth out in the sink. There was another knock on the door.

"What bitch?"

"It's Malcolm. Is he ready?"

Marek went to secure the door but Mallory grabbed his arm and held him back. He walked toward the door and opened it slowly. Malcolm stood there. Mallory stood face-to-face with his father and their eyes locked. Malcolm gazed deeply into his eyes and noticed the change in color. Although this frightened him a bit, he never lost his strong expression.

Uncle Mal walked up and patted Mallory on the shoulder. "Are you ready, son?"

Mallory didn't move until Malcolm finally blinked. Mallory took a deep breath and then walked off. Malcolm bowed his head down. The tables were about to turn for Mallory.

The wedding party was in position; however, Mallory walked past everyone down the aisle. Once he got to the altar, he sat down on the step. Everyone was baffled. The musicians started playing and the groomsmen escorted their bridesmaids' out beautifully. Mallory looked behind him and noticed a door that led to the groom's room. He got up and walked behind the altar and back into the room. His brothers, who were on the first pew, didn't realize that he left. The flower girl threw her rose petals down the aisle. Everyone's eyes followed her gracefully until they reached the altar and they noticed that Mallory was gone.

"Fuck! Where is he?" Marc tried to get out of the pew but Marek held him back. It was too late.

Everyone stood up to salute the bride. Escorted by her father, Stacy gracefully walked down the aisle in her sterling white tulle wedding ball gown. The organizer fussed over the cathedral length veil to ensure that her presence was flawless. Malcolm and the others feverishly looked around for Mallory. Once she reached the last pew, Mallory appeared, walking from behind the altar and down the isle. He stood in front of her father and grabbed her hand, saluting his beautiful princess.

"Is he supposed to do that?" Marlon asked.

"NO!" Marc shouted quietly. The music stopped.

"Stacy," Mallory kissed her hand. "Will you marry me? I didn't ask you before. I think it's rather rude for me to think that you would and I didn't ask you."

"Yes, Mallory," Stacy smiled.

He escorted her to the altar, leaving her confused father behind. The minister started speaking and everyone quieted down.

Mallory gazed upon Stacy admiring her innocence and angelic presence. "You're so beautiful."

"Thank you," she smiled.

"You're a princess, an angelical princess."

"Mallory, the minister is speaking. Shh..." Stacy interrupted him.

"MINISTER? As in a man of God?" He turned to the minister and shouted, "Are you a man of God?"

Malcolm's lips motioned "NO" to the minister and the minister reluctantly whispered "no." The minister continued the wedding monologue but Mallory interrupted him again.

"What are you saying?" He turned toward Stacy. "What's he saying, princess?"

"He's saying our vows."

"Why?"

"So we can repeat them."

"You don't know them? You don't know what you will vow to me?" Mallory said boldly.

She paused to think but didn't answer.

"I do. I vow to honor you and protect you. I vow to admire you. I vow sheer ecstasy and ultimate intimacy. I vow my life. I can love ...will enjoy ...every moment of your life and thereafter." He kneeled down placing the ring on her finger. "I vow my heart and soul to you." He kissed her hand.

She smiled and lifted his face up. "I vow my chastity, honesty and loyalty. I will love you and only you. You're my highest and no one shall separate us. I vow my heart and soul."

Sniffles broke the silence in the room. After moments of awkward silence, the minister interjected, "I now pronounce you husband and wife?"

Mallory shot him death looks.

"You may kiss your bride." The minister smiled nervously.

Mallory gently wrapped his arms around her waist and kissed her softly. However, the kiss became so overwhelming that she fainted in his arms and the crowd gasped. He sat her down on his lap and waited for her to awaken. When she finally came to, she started crying. "Don't cry princess. What's wrong?"

"I can't do this! I don't know you. I'm so scared. I don't know what or how to..."

"Don't cry. You'll mess up your beautiful face," Mallory shook his head. "A ten-year difference and we finally have something in common. I'm scared and confused too. I don't know what to do myself. But we'll figure this out together. Don't be afraid of me, I won't hurt you. I promise."

She laid her head on his shoulder.

"Are you ready, Mrs. Mallory Haulm?"

"Yes, Mr. Haulm."

𝔐

The door to the hotel suite swung open and hit the wall, blasting an echo through the dark empty room. They looked at each other with lost expressions. Mallory bowed his head and motioned for Stacy to walk in first. He was more nervous than Stacy, as she stood in the middle of the suite, scared and waiting for directions. For the first time in his life, Mallory had no desire to have sex. He walked over to the suite bar and pulled out several mini bottles of Vodka. He opened one right after the other and started shooting them. He caught a glance of her in mid-shot.

She's going to think that I'm an alcoholic. Misery loves company! He asked invitingly. "Do you want one?"

"Yeah, but I can't drink."

"Why not?"

"Age, duh."

"Married ... celebration ... honeymoon ... duh?" He mimicked her.

She laughed and walked over toward him.

"I can vouch for you drinking tonight. What do you want?"

She hunched her shoulders.

"You like sweet?"

"Yeah."

He selected an Amaretto. "Do you like cough syrup?"

"What?"

"Nothing," he laughed. "Here, try this one with ice." He put a couple of cubes in a glass and handed to her.

"What are you drinking?"

"Vodka. It's a hard drink. Lesson one about drinking; never mix dark liquors with lights." She sipped her drink slowly.

"That's what Daddy says about races."

"Your Daddy is a prick. So if he doesn't like black people, why did he make you marry me?"

"He says that your family transcends race."

"Oh," Mallory thought back to his newfound identity.

"Do you know what that means?"

"No, but when I figure it out I'll let you know," he winked. "I'm going to take a shower," he said as his passed her, being careful not to touch her.

She smiled and cradled her drink close to her bosom. She attempted to sit on the couch, but had a difficult time with her wedding dress. Mallory sighed. The last thing he wanted to do was touch her.

"Do you need help with that dress?"

"M-hum." She turned and he started unbuttoning her dress.

He felt her tremble with every touch. He tried hard not to let his fingers touch her body but the dress was tailored to melt onto her. With each touch, he felt sick and dizzy. "How many buttons do you have on this bloody thing?"

"Thirty-nine, I think. One button for every year you were alive." She snickered.

Her comment caught him below the belt and he laughed. As his laughter settled his nausea, he kissed her at the nape of her neck. "Cute! Finish your drink, I'll be back." He walked to the bathroom and locked the door. He picked up his cell phone to call Matthew. "Hey, I need to talk to you. I miss you. And you were right; I did regret not walking you out. Call me, please. I love you."

He sat on the floor for a while holding the phone. He finally undressed and climbed in the shower. He sat in the shower until the water ran cold. He slowly dried off his body and walked into the bedroom. Without thinking, he put his dress pants back on leaving his pajamas on the bed. He walked out to see that she was wearing bridal lingerie. Once again, she looked and felt out of place.

"Your mom's underwear?"

"No, I bought it," she said defensively.

Mallory rolled his eyes

"But my mom helped pick it out."

"Do you really want to wear that?"

"Not really."

"Go get comfortable, please?"

With her head bowed like a little child, she walked back into the bedroom.

He walked toward the suite bar and noticed that there were a couple of more empty bottles. "She's going to get drunk. That's all I need is a drunk virgin." He grabbed bottled water instead. He sauntered to the couch and flopped down.

She finally walked out the bedroom with a skimpy nightshirt with "THREE some" plastered across her chest and boy short shorts.

"I like that." Mallory grabbed for her hand.

"Really? I thought of you when I saw it. Mom thought it would put you off."

"Did you tell your mom that you called me a faggot in public?"

"No!"

"Well, if that didn't put me off, nothing will." Mallory kissed her fingertips. She flopped down next to him. She still looked as if she was still waiting for instructions. "Do you want to watch a movie?"

"Yeah," She snatched the remote and starting switching channels. "Oh, 'The Bird Cage!' I love this movie. I think Nathan Lane is awesome."

Mallory laid back vaguely watching the movie. The actors were different but this movie was similar to Matthew's favorite French movie. This revelation made Mallory miss him more. He moved back, allowing her to lie with him. He tried hard to get himself in the mood by removing pins from her hair. Each curl he unpinned, he felt nauseous. She turned around and kissed him boldly.

"What was that for?" Mallory pushed her back.

"Isn't that what I'm supposed to do?"

"If you want to but,"

"Have you ever had sex with a woman?"

He paused in embarrassment. "Women. Not girls."

"I'm not a damn girl."

"Okay ... let's try another word. Experienced, not virgins."

She looked down.

"I don't want to fight with you. Although this is a safe place because no one can hear us."

"Mom said I'm supposed to give myself to you."

"Do you know what that means?"

"Yeah, I'm supposed to let you fuck me."

"Damn." He looked offended.

"I want to get it over with."

"What?"

"You're acting weird. I thought maybe you're used to women coming onto you or don't you know how to do it because you're gay."

"Stop this madness." He shot up off the couch and walked to the bar. "I'll have you know I make my own advances. I have slept with only one man." He stepped back shouting. "Can I tell you the truth?" Mallory wanted to tell her how much he missed Matthew and how he wanted to smell his scent, feel his strong arms around him. He wanted to grab all his heat. He decided not to. "It has been a long time since I've been with a woman. You're right; I don't know what to do." That was the first time he ever lied about sex.

"That's okay. My mom says that the first time sucks anyway."

"She told you that?"

Stacy nodded her head.

"How sad?"

"Did your first time suck?" she asked.

Mallory couldn't respond right away. He couldn't decide which first time. Michelle or Matthew. "No, it was great."

"It's always great for the guy."

"Not always." He decided to mix the stories. "My first time, I threw up on the ... girl."

"Really?"

"Yes, I was so embarrassed."

"What happened?"

"We did it again. It was great. I guess the first time does suck. But it doesn't have to."

She grabbed his hand and led him to the bedroom. When she jumped in the bed, he looked at her strangely. "Let's get it over with."

"Don't you want to enjoy it?"

"My mom says that I'll get a better thrill if I do it myself."

"Your mom is a suffering woman. I feel for her."

"I guess. Come on."

Stacy lay lifeless in the bed. Mallory forced himself to make a move by crawling in the bed slowly. He kissed her softly and slowly and she began relaxing and responding. As he caressed her gently, he laid down on her and she tensed up. *This is not going to work*, he thought. "Hey why don't you get on top?" He flipped onto his back and she straddled him.

They started kissing again and he grabbed her body, rubbing and squeezing her slowly, and she responded again. He slipped his hand inside her shorts and she tensed up again. He held his arms up and away from her body.

She laid her head down on his chest. "I'm sorry."

"No worries," he huffed and looked aimlessly at the ceiling. "Throw some clothes on and let's get out of here. This hotel room is intimidating."

She flew off the bed, grabbing his jacket and then flew out of the room. Mallory crawled out slowly, grabbing his cell phone and calling Matthew, but he still didn't answer. He grudgingly stood up, grabbed his shirt and met her in the living room.

As they walked off the elevator, they spotted Malcolm and the senator standing at the entrance engaged in an intensive discussion. Those were the last two people Mallory wanted to see. He grabbed her arm and whispered, "Let's escape." They ducked behind a column, and then ran out the exit door. As they ran toward Mallory's car, they broke out in laughter. "So do you want to go any place in particular?"

"I don't know," she said as she jumped in the car. She went to close the door, but she cut her finger on a piece of glass. "Ouch!"

"What's wrong?"

"I cut my finger."

Mallory grabbed her finger and examined it. He looked around for a cloth to wipe her cut but then he remembered the ritual. He closed his eyes and gently placed her finger in his mouth. He kissed her finger and said, "I know a great spot."

He started the car and put it in reverse. They drove away in silence, avoiding any eye contact. Every so often, Mallory could feel her staring at him, so he would look over and flash a reassuring smile.

They finally arrived at the spot where he and Matthew had their first outing as a couple, the lake. Mallory loved the lake. It was secluded and serene. If nothing else, at least he was with Matthew in spirit. He found his favorite spot to park.

"I like this." She smiled.

"I do too. It's quiet and tranquil, but we can be as loud as we want."

"Really?"

"Sure."

"Turn on some music," she said as she jumped out of the car.

Mallory opened the convertible top of his BMW and turned on the music. He flashed his high beams on Stacy as she danced to all of his rap and neo soul music. He got out of the car and sat on the hood, admiring her. She was having a great time. It turned out to be a wonderful idea to come to the lake and remove all the expectations to perform.

"Sing to me!" she shouted.

"Why?"

"I like your voice."

"I think we'll have to listen to something old for that." He got back in the car and searched for a song. He remembered the song Matthew played for him when they were out there. If he's not here in person, he'll be here in spirit. "Do you know Luther?"

"I think so. My mom said I was conceived off one of his songs."

"Hopefully not the song I'm choosing."

She laughed.

The beginning of 'Make me a Believer' rang out across the lake. He sat back on the hood, closed his eyes and started singing. Stacy danced around the car. After the second chorus, she decided to crawl on the hood and sit in his lap. His eyes opened as he smiled at her. She kissed him innocently. He gently grabbed her waist and held her body close to him. He started grinding her gently. There was no resistance this time. He lifted his body with one arm and looked deeply into her eyes. "Are you ready?"

"I think so," she whispered.

"Don't fight me. Just tell me if you don't like it."

She nodded.

"You'll enjoy this, I promise." He kissed her again, but harder and more intense. He removed her boy shorts and she wrapped her legs around his waist. She boldly unzipped his pants and pulled out his hot throbbing penis. He grabbed her hand, and helped her fiercely stroke his penis, gliding it along the side of her leg. He could feel her shiver. "Don't ... don't think. Just breathe." He took a deep breath and gradually entered her. With each gentle stroke, he could feel Stacy holding her breath. "Breathe, Stacy, breathe, baby ... breathe ..." It felt like an eternity, but he managed to enter her completely and slowly without her tensing up. "Do something for me?"

"If I touch something that drives you crazy, let me know."

She nodded again.

He started grinding her slowly but intensely. Her body responded and she mimicked his motion. He felt her body communicating with him so he knew that it was a good time to change position. He lifted her up and laid back on the hood with her on top. "You find the spot and I'll guide you."

She grabbed his chest and started moving her hips in circles. He grabbed the top of the hood and pulled them up. He positioned his feet on the bumper so they wouldn't fall. He and Matthew learned that trick. He closed his eyes and imagined the many times he was with Matthew to keep his erection. He grabbed her hips and guided her through her first orgasm. She collapsed on his body and he kissed her forehead. She rose up and smiled.

"How was it?" he asked.

"Better than I imagined."

"Excellent," he ran his fingertips down her neck and back as she rested her head on his chest. She gently kissed his chest and ran circles around his nipples with her tongue. She eventually sat back up and grinned. "Wanna do it again?" He entangled a lock of her hair between his fingers.

"Yeah."

"You want to stay this way?"

She nodded.

"Go for it."

She sat back up and resumed her grinding motion. Mallory was still distant from the whole event. He saw himself in a bad movie; not a porn flick, but one of those independent films Matthew loved to watch. She was right, the first time with her sucked. He felt no connection with her.

What started out as tears became rain that ran down his face. They both jumped off the hood and ran to the passenger side of the car. She jumped in the back and Mallory started the car and pressed the button to close the top. They looked at each other and laughed. He pulled her from the back seat to the passenger seat and she resumed her quest.

"I can love you if you want me to," she said innocently.

"I would like that," he forced a response as he kissed her intensely, grabbing and squeezing her hips firmly. As she came again, this time tears falling from her eyes. Mallory looked away in embarrassment. He held her body close to his to help him fight back the nausea that was building inside.

Mallory woke up crunched down in the passenger seat with Stacy entangled in his lap. He tried to move, but he felt his body aching. Gliding his hand across the door, he searched for the latch and opened the door. He untangled himself from Stacy and got out of the car.

That's why we took the truck," he thought. There is no way two men can work that out in the back seat of a car.

He walked over to the other side of the car, jumped in, and started the car. When he looked over, he saw that Stacy was wearing his tuxedo shirt and nothing else. So, he popped the trunk and pulled out the felt car cover. He got back in and covered her up. Since he was minutes from his house, he decided to drive home.

Driving up to his driveway, he noticed that she was still asleep. He walked to the front door and opened it, then went back to the car, scooped up her fragile body and carried her to his bedroom and placed her on the bed. He walked to the kitchen and grabbed bottled water. He returned to the bedroom and sat on the bed watching her sleep. She looked so small and fragile and even more innocent than she did last night. The nausea rose again but Mallory lost the battle of keeping it down. He ran to the bathroom and slid across the floor on his knees barely making it to the bowl. He threw up repeatedly, until his energy was gone.

He barely had enough strength to crawl over to the phone. He picked it up to call Matthew, but there was still no answer. He hung up the phone and crawled in the shower. He turned on the highest setting. It was the second time in two weeks that he used that setting. He screamed as the piercing shots of burning water bounced off his body.

After an hour passed, he finally got out of the shower and dried himself off. He walked back into the bedroom and saw that Stacy had left the bed. When he walked into the kitchen, he saw Stacy talking with Peter.

"I see you have met my wife." Mallory said, walking up to the bar.

"Yes, she's a lovely soul." Peter commented with a smile.

"I was looking for you," Stacy said. "Mr. Peter said you were in the shower and probably wanted to be alone."

"Yes, that's my private space. Did you want to take a shower?"

"I did, in the other room. Mr. Peter said that room would be mine."

"I guess if you don't want to sleep with me." He chuckled as he sat next to her. "It's nice to have your own room, and you can fix it up however you like."

"Thanks," she said quietly while bouncing around in her seat.

There was a long awkward silence. Mallory picked at the granite on his bar and she swirled nervously in her seat. Peter tried engaging them in conversation but neither one would extend the conversation further than a one- or two-word comment. They all sighed relief when the phone rang.

Peter answered it quickly, "Haulm residence. Mallory?"

Mallory fiercely shook his head no.

"No, sir, Mallory is not available. Have you tried him on the cell phone? You have? The phone is at the hotel?" He frowned. "I'm sure they'll be back soon, sir. Maybe they went to breakfast. Yes, sir. When I see him, I'll let him know. Thank you."

"I'm sorry that I had you lie."

"I didn't lie. You're not available. You are busy attending to your new wife." Peter winked.

Mallory gave in to the battle that he was married. He flashed a fake grin and wrapped his arms around Stacy then said, "Let's get back."

"What's next?"

"Well, let's see. We're both adults," Mallory paused; "At least I am ..." he teased. "What do you want to do next?"

She laid her head on his shoulders and stared at the ceiling.

"Let's start with the obvious. What was disrupted by this marriage?"

"Your relationship with Matthew?"

"I was thinking you and school. Do you want to finish school?" She nodded. "Let's work on getting you back in school, and we will have plenty of time to start whatever ..." Mallory refused to say the word family.

"Don't you want children?"

"Does this house look child-friendly to you?" Mallory shouted.

She took a close look around the room as he shouted again.

"Do I look child friendly to you? You should know by experience that I'm not. We can wait on that. We can definitely wait ... a long, long, long time."

"So, you will let me go back to school?"

"Absolutely! You're going back to school, even if Peter has to drive you himself." He winked at Peter.

CHAPTER THIRTEEN

As they drove up to the hotel entrance, they saw a crowd of people waiting for them. Mallory decided to park his own car. When they walked in the hotel, Stacy spotted her mother and ran to her like a lost little girl. Marc and Marek spotted him nonchalantly strolling toward the hotel café.

"Where were you?" Marc confronted him.

"Out!"

"Where, Mallory?"

"Look, just because I married a nineteen-year-old doesn't give you the right to treat me like I'm nineteen. I'm grown. Recognize that!" He stormed off.

"We know," Marek pushed Marc aside and caught up with Mallory. "Remember what I said?"

"Yes, is 11:57 okay with you? She cut her finger." Mallory walked into the café and found a table. "Can I have Earl Grey tea and a shot of espresso?"

Marc and Marek sat down across from him. Mallory felt Marc's eyes burning in his skin. He decided that, unless Marc asked him a question, he wasn't going to acknowledge him.

Stacy strolled in and stood next to him. "I need the key to get my things."

He patted his pockets and retrieved the card key. "When are you leaving?"

"Tomorrow afternoon."

"Excellent! I might come up to NY later and surprise you," Mallory said as he winked at her.

"Where's she going?" Marc inquired.

"Back to school."

"Why?" Marc shouted.

"That's what we agree upon. Stop!" He held his hand to Marc's face, stopping him in mid-sentence, and stood up. "Stacy, you have a great trip back. Call me when you get there, okay?" She stuck her hand out for him to kiss it. He smiled as she bounced back to her mom, and they walked away.

In one smooth move, Mallory's smiled disappeared and he leaned over Marc and shouted. "Just because you forced me to marry her doesn't give you any authority to run my marriage. Stay the fuck out of my business, or you'll regret it."

Marek jumped up and tried to separate them. "Cool. You married her, you did her, and we're done with that."

"No, we're not. That's not how it's done."

"That's how I'm doing it." Mallory's beverages came in separate cups. He combined his tea with the shot and took big gulps to calm his nerves. He sat back down and took several deep breaths.

"You're so stupid. She needs to be with you. You don't let her go tramping off!"

"Tramping off! Did you ever stop to think that I want an intelligent woman, not some bitch in heat that lies around popping out puppies?"

"Fuck you, Mallory. At least I'm fucking something that can produce!" Marc leaned in to antagonize him. "Was it hard for you to hit that? How long did it take? Could you even get it up? Or did you have to tap that ass?"

Mallory threw his tea then the cup at Marc and stormed off.

"Marc, you need to stop," Marek said.

"Fuck that faggot. He gets on my fucking nerves." Marc said as he wiped his face.

"Do you ever stop to think that you get on his fucking nerves?"

"Whose side are you on?"

"Mine bitch! I mean, damn, Marc. He did almost everything he was supposed to do. All we have to do is guide him through the next stage. Why are you riding his ass?"

"Watch your words." Marc stormed off. Marek shook his head and followed him.

Mallory stormed off the elevator toward the room. He grabbed the door just as Stacy and her mom opened it to leave. She held the door open for him. They decided to stay awhile after watching him storm through door and collapse on the couch. She kneeled down in front of him and planted her elbows on his knees. "I told my mom about you."

His mouth flew open.

"She was excited. She said few men can achieve that ... first time being great and all."

"Excellent. I'm glad you enjoyed it." Mallory said nervously. "I told you that you would."

There was a strong knock on the door, Stacy's mom quickly ran to answer it. Marc boldly walked into the room and Marek followed closely.

"How are you doing, Mother Silverman? You're looking gorgeous today." Marc gently placed a hand on each of her shoulders and kissed both cheeks.

"Thank you, Marc. How is your father?"

"He's well. He asks about you all the time. I wanted to tell you that we're having a family dinner tonight. You must come," Marc announced.

"Stacy needs to go home and pack," Mallory protested.

"She needs to come and meet her new family. We Haulms are sticklers for rituals." Marc gently grabbed her hands. "Please come. We would love to have you there."

"Marc, she needs to pack for school." Mallory stood up and raised his voice this time.

"We'll be there ... maybe for a little while," the mother said with a smile, as she grabbed her arm and escorted her out.

Mallory made a beeline for the bedroom, slamming the door behind him. He picked up his cell phone off the bed and called Matthew again, but there was still no answer. He left another message, "You're making me feel like a stalker. Please call me, please. I really need to hear your voice." Mallory quickly hung up the phone when Marc walked in.

"Who are you calling?"

Mallory didn't answer.

"Your little faggot ass boyfriend. You know that you have to let that nasty shit go." Mallory looked down. "You're a fucking Haulm, and we don't need any faggots in our family."

"Like it or not, you got one."

"Not if I can change it."

"What are you going to do? Harass me to death." Mallory charged up to him

"Kill you if I have to." Marc pushed him back.

Marek rushed in. "Marc stop. You don't mean that."

"What makes you think that you can kill me? Malcolm couldn't."

"I'm not Dad. I finish my shit."

"Well finish it." Mallory charged up to Marc again and they were inches from each other, ready to fight.

Marek tried pushing them apart. "Look, stop. Let's just go." Marek pleaded.

"Dad was right ... mom should have aborted you."

Mallory dropped his head and stepped back.

"You were a waste —" Before Marc could finish his statement, Mallory smashed his cell phone across Marc's head. Marc fell back and Mallory started hitting him in his chest and face. Marek tried holding him back, but he was flipped over during the scuffle.

Marc finally got his balance and lunged after Mallory but slipped through Marc's grasp and pushed him against the wall. Marc pushed back and hit Mallory across his face. He attempted to plant an upper cut but Mallory deflected it, hitting Marc in the abdomen. Marc attempted to return the body blow but Mallory grabbed his arm and threw him up against the wall again.

When Marek tried to break it up again, they all fell on the bed. Marc broke free and turned over on Mallory. He went to punch Mallory, but Mallory deflected it and Marc hit Marek in the face. Mallory kicked him in the abdomen. Marek managed to hold Mallory down, begging and pleading for them to stop.

Marc regained his stance and stood over him, unzipping his pants. "I AM the leader. I AM the head honcho ... the big dick, not you. You want to see a big dick, boy?" He pulled out his penis and urinated on Mallory. "You need to be put in your place."

Marek let Mallory go.

Mallory jumped up, grabbed Marc, swirling him around and pulling his pants down the rest of the way.

"You wanted me this whole fucking time," Mallory shouted as they struggled. Mallory crushed his head into the television and Marc fell back. He was hurt and disoriented. Mallory grabbed him and threw him on the bed. "I think that you're mad because you're not the brother that I'm fucking!"

Marek tried to hold Mallory back, but Mallory flung Marek across the room.

"If you wanted me, all you had to do was ask." He straddled him and unzipped his pants.

"Mallory, don't do it," Marek pleaded.

"No Marek, he wants this. He's wanted this since I got back. Is that the reason you did Amanda? That's what you wanted, to do me?" he shouted. He planted his knee in Marc's back then placed one arm down on the side of Marc and bent down, stroking his penis.

"Mallory," Marek stood up and decided not to stop him physically. He pleaded calmly, "You don't want to do this. You keep saying that what you and Matthew have is special. And you love him, right? You know he wouldn't want you to do this."

"I don't give a fuck what Matthew wants." Mallory shouted as he punched Marc in the head.

"Yeah you do. You love him, right?"

Mallory sat up and looked at Marek.

"You know if you go through with this ... this will make you a faggot, a sick faggot for real. You don't want that. You don't want the memories of what you and Matthew shared to be tainted by this bitch move. Don't let this jackass fuck up what you have with Matty." That last statement caught Mallory's attention. That was the first time he heard anyone refer to Matthew by his pet name.

Mallory got up and zipped his pants. He walked out of the room and sat on the couch.

Marc rolled over in the bed and Marek handed him his pants and helped him up. "This is the last time I save your ass. Next time, I'm holding your legs. Leave him alone."

Marc sat on the bed and tried to regain his composure.

Marek slowly walked into the living area and sat next to Mallory. He handed him his cell phone. "Call him."

Mallory sat up and called him again. This time Matthew answered. "Hey, baby, I have been calling you. Did you get my messages?"

"Yes," he said abruptly.

"What's wrong?"

There was a long pause. "Emerald, I can't talk right now." He snapped back.

"Okay?" Tears started building in Mallory's eyes. He wanted to ask Matthew so many questions. *Are you mad at me? Do you still love me? Are we okay?* He just wanted Matthew's tone to change so he could receive a sign that everything was fine. "Matty ..."

"I'll call you back."

Mallory's words were choking him. "Matty, I ..."

"Goodbye, Emerald."

Mallory couldn't get himself to say goodbye.

The phone clicked. He couldn't remember Matthew ever saying goodbye. He handed the phone back to Marek. He got up and left the hotel room.

After wandering around in the garage, Mallory walked to his car and got in slowly. He didn't know where to go. His head was filled with anger, pain and confusion. He started his car and put the car in reverse, backing up then suddenly stopping. He put the car in park and jumped out. "I could have run over you."

"You think?" The French voice said rudely. He looked down. She walked up to him and grabbed his face. "Why do I see you every time you are at a crossroads?"

"I don't know."

"Come with me."

They arrived at to Brielle's loft. Although Brielle got out, Mallory stayed in the car for a long time. He eventually crawled out of the car and walked to the door. He pushed the door open to see Brielle sitting on the floor waiting for him. Mallory bowed his head and walked toward the couch. He was a shattered shell. His father hated him; his oldest brother rejected him for reasons he didn't understand. He was forced to marry a girl who had no idea who he was. He didn't understand who he was either. Most of all, he lost the love of his life, the reason he wanted to exist.

Brielle knew how fragile he was. She felt each explosion blowing up inside of him; how every pain he relived broke him apart. She wanted to help him shed his anger and pain, not for his sake but for the world's sake. As she sat next to him, she waited for a sign to comfort him. The first tear finally fell and she was relieved. She grabbed him and held him close. He broke down and sobbed in her arms. She didn't need to know the details because she felt the pain.

She was summoned to catch him before he fell. The world wasn't ready for him to fall. She rocked him slowly and silently, stroking his hair. He finally looked up in her eyes. She placed his head in her bosom and rocked him again. She felt some of the tension leave his body. She held his face again and kissed his tears, then his lips.

"Even gods cry," she whispered.

He kissed her back and they both felt that familiar spark. After awhile, she broke the kiss and grabbed his face again. "You're better than this. You deserve better than this. If you knew who you were, you wouldn't be here. You wouldn't feel this pain. You are a God. You command all of life. Accept it. Just accept it."

"I don't know how."

"I'll help you. Will you let me help you?"

"I'm not ready."

"Fine, I'll be here when you're ready." She wrapped her arms around him. "Let's have some wine." She got up and disappeared into the other room.

Mallory looked around and noticed another life-size canvas. The picture was of the same man he saw before, but the man appeared to be drowning. The torrential waves swelled up to his knees, and bodies were drowning and floating around him. He starting hearing loud screams. He covered his ears and closed his eyes, but the screams grew louder.

She reappeared, "drink this." When he opened his eyes, the noise stopped.

"This is red wine. I usually don't drink red wine."

"And you're usually unhappy," she said as she disappeared out of the room again. He took a big sip of the red wine and closed his eyes. He laid back on the couch, rubbing his eyes. He felt his body separate from itself.

She reappeared with a blank life-size canvas and placed it in front of him. She sat back in his lap and handed him another glass of wine. "Drink, my love."

With his eyes still closed, he gulped down the entire glass of wine. His body began tearing in two. He opened his eyes and saw himself floating away and onto the canvas. There were big splashes of harsh dark rainbow paints hitting against the canvas.

"What time is it?" Mallory decided not to question her art.

"8 o'clock."

"Shit, I have a dinner party."

"Mallory, stay with me."

"I said I would be there."

"As you wish," she released him and he stood up.

"Do you want to come?" He stood over her, stroking her hair.

"Is that wise?"

"I don't care about wise. I want you there." He gently grabbed her hair, pulling her back and kissing her.

"Let me get dressed."

"I need to get dressed, too. I'll go to the office and I'll be back here in an hour."

ℳ

Mallory's drive to the office was a flash. He was so preoccupied playing back the last day's events that he was in front of his building before he knew it. The strangest part was he felt no emotions. He double parked in front of the building and entered with a fierce walk.

"You're here late," the security guard said as his presence frightened her.

"I forgot something. Watch my car," he said harshly and rushed to the elevator. He forcefully pushed his office door open and pulled off his clothes. He walked past his desk and saw his message light blinking. He turned on his computer and checked the message. It was from Matthew. He started the message.

"Hey Emerald," there was a long pause. "I think we need to talk."

"Bloody hell! He's leaving me." Mallory stopped listening to the message and walked into the shower.

The message continued, "Baby, I'm sorry. Some things ... new discoveries have gotten me fucked up here. I need some time to figure this out." There was another pause then his tone softened. "I know that you're worried about us. We're okay, I-I think. I love you, baby, and I miss you too, and I'm not mad. I miss your touch. Hearing your voice just makes me...I miss you so much." His tone changed again. "I need figure this out, but this is my last trip, I promise. It's so fucked up, Emerald. I'll be home soon. I hope you had a beautiful wedding. Oh ... EM I didn't mean bye, I meant good night. Good night baby."

"Have you seen Mallory?" Marc walked in the kitchen to find Marek shooting gin. Marek rolled his eyes but didn't answer. "I don't know why you're so mad. He whooped my ass."

"I wonder why. I still owe you a punch, bitch. And you're dry cleaning my shit. Where the fuck do you get off pissing on somebody?" Marek charged up to Marc just when Malcolm walked into the heated discussion.

"I guess they're right. Faggots are strong," Marc said.

Marek pushed him up against the wall. "You got one more time to call him a faggot."

"Stop it!" Malcolm pulled them apart. "What's going on?"

Marek walked off and didn't answer.

"We're looking for Mallory," Marc answered while straightening his clothes.

"No we're not. He said he would be here. I'm not worried."

"He's in the living room," Malcolm said.

"Good! I have..." Marc started for the door.

"You leave him alone. I'm warning you. I'm not covering your ass this time."

"I don't need you to cover my ass."

"Oh really! It didn't look like that today at the hotel." Marek started for the door. "Leave him alone. Don't go near him. That's my final warning." He walked out.

"What's going on?" Malcolm asked again.

"Every one thinks that Mallory is so fragile and so soft that he needs to be protected. If that's the case, let's kill him. We don't need him, Dad." He grabbed his father's arms. "He's weakening us, Dad. I can do both charges. We don't need him."

"I understand what you're saying, but you're the leader of this family. You can't do all three. I need you to lead this family. Mallory is confused for some reason. I'll figure out why he is acting this way, but I need you to lead this family."

"How can he not know? He was with Uncle Mal. Uncle Mal was the teacher in the family. I can't believe that he didn't teach Mallory personally. He taught us."

Malcolm tried sidetracking Marc's questions regarding Mallory. "I don't know. I need to speak with Uncle Mal about that, okay? But let's assume that he doesn't know."

"I can't do that. That would really put us in a weak position. We would have to start with Horseman 101. Dad, I can't do that!"

"Marc, you're a strong leader. You command this family. Give Mallory the benefit of the doubt. He is a quick learner ... if he doesn't respond," he paused. "We'll go some other options."

"Good!"

"Marc, give him a fighting chance before you do anything." Marc huffed then walked out of the kitchen.

Mallory and Brielle slipped into the party unnoticed. Once they walked in, they went in separate directions. Mallory walked around looking for his brothers so he could check in. He unknowingly passed Stacy and didn't acknowledge her.

She quickly grabbed his arm, "Mallory?"

"Stacy?" he said with no feeling.

"I'm glad you made it. I was about to leave. Some of my friends are going to the movies, and I wanted to go."

"Then go..." He walked off and she followed him. He spotted Marek and headed in his direction. "Marek, I'm here. I said that I would be here." He said between breaths.

"Man, you don't look right?" Marek examined Mallory closely. His eyes were blood shot and dilated. He was sweating and his skin was clammy. He had a hard time focusing on Marek.

"I'm fine. I think I need to go to the loo." His eyes drifted off in space. "Yes, I do. Where is it?" He walked off again and Stacy went to follow him, but Marek stopped her.

"Stay at the party, I'll check on him."

Marek finally found Mallory walking into the hall bathroom and followed him in. "I can pee by myself."

"You're not acting right. What's wrong?" He posted Mallory against the wall.

"I'm fine. Where's Marc? I can't zip my pants?"

Marek left out a huge sigh. "Tuck your shit in ..." He reluctantly grabbed the flap and quickly zipped them. "I don't think you want to see Marc." He straightened his shirt then shook his face. "Look at me!"

"Yes, I want him to know that I'm here. I love him so much. I don't know why he hates me. Everyone hates me." Mallory pushed him away and sat on the toilet. "You know I can't find my cell phone. I know that Matthew's trying to call me." Mallory kept rambling.

"Mallory, you broke the cell phone on Marc's head."

"I did? I'm so sorry." He shot up and headed for the door. "I need to apologize. He's going be mad at me."

Marek stopped him from leaving. "No, you don't want to do that."

"Why?"

"He deserved it."

"No he didn't. He's a good guy. I'm so screwed up. I'm a faggot. I'm a fucking loser." Mallory was disoriented again. "I can't find my cell phone." He started searching his pockets for his phone. "I know that Matthew is trying to call me."

There was a knock and Marek answered, "It's occupied!"

"Mallory?" Brielle called out.

"Let her in ... Let her in." Mallory rushed to the door again. Marek pushed him out of the way but reluctantly opened the door. Brielle entered slowly and Mallory grabbed her, putting her on the counter.

"You brought her here?" Marek protested.

"Yes. Isn't she beautiful? I want her."

"Mallory, this is a bad..." Before he could finish his statement, he was posted up against the door by Brielle's petite foot. Brielle's toes were crawling up his leg. They finally stopped between his legs and started massaging his crouch. She grabbed Mallory's face and started kissing him and nibbling on his neck.

"Can I have her, Marek? Please?" Mallory begged but Marek was speechless.

Marek couldn't move and really didn't want to.

Brielle jumped off the counter and backed into Marek, grabbing Mallory to follow her. She whispered to Marek, "Besides it should be you I'm doing this to... I was your *real* intended. But I guess you don't remember that... I guess ALL HAULM MEN have blackouts!"

Marek didn't get what she was saying until he remembered his pen pal from college. *Elizabeth Liveoak.* His heart sank. That was his true love, his intended wife. With everything that was going on during that time with his father and trying to get into the Marines, she fell by the wayside. That was Marek's one true regret, not fighting his family hard enough to marry Elizabeth.

"Please, Marek? Can I?" Mallory looked at her as if she were the only one in the room. She started grinding Marek.

"He asked you a question. I think it's rude if you don't answer," Brielle said softly. "At least he can enjoy the fun."

Mallory started kissing her on the arms and neck. "Can I, Marek, please?" He continued to beg. "Can I, Marek, please?"

Marek grabbed her hips in an attempt to push her away but she moved them more forcefully, so he finally gave in. When he finally came, he wrapped his arms around her and whispered, "I'm sorry, baby. Forgive me."

There was another knock at the door and they all jumped. It was Marc. "Mallory, are you in there?" Marc asked through the door as he jingled the knob.

Mallory started to speak but Marek covered his mouth. "Nawh, man, I'm in here." Marek answered, "Check the kitchen."

"I went to the kitchen."

"Check the cellar."

"Yeah, the faggot likes to drink wine," Marc said.

Mallory slumped back.

"Marc, I warned you," Marek shouted through the door.

"Sorry. Look if you see the little bitch tell him that I'm looking for him. We need to talk about tomorrow. Since everybody wants to treat him special, I wanna be there to tell him about the next stage. So don't tell him anything until we see him together, alright?"

Mallory sat back on the toilet.

Brielle walked to him to comfort him. "Let's go home, baby." She grabbed his hand and he got up, holding his head down.

Marek opened the door and let them out. He placed his hand on Mallory's shoulders as tears fell from Mallory's eyes, though he never looked up. They walked down the stairs and Marek followed them out. As Brielle passed a server, she grabbed a champagne glass from the tray.

They finally reached the outside and she put Mallory in the car. He felt emptier than before. Before she walked over to the driver side, she retrieved her purse and pulled out a small pouch. She placed the contents of the pouch in the champagne glass and handed the glass to Mallory.

"Drink, my love." He took a big gulp and threw the glass on the ground. She got in the car and as she sped off, Marc appeared at the entrance door.

"Mallory! MALLORY!" Marc ran out the house toward Marek, shouting. Brielle flew past them, barely missing Marc.

"Marek, who was that?" Marc shouted but Marek shook his head and then walked away. "Marek, did you tell him about tomorrow? MAREK!"

CHAPTER FOURTEEN

Brielle finally reached the loft. She opened the door and grabbed his hand. She took him below the stairs, to a room in the loft he had never been in before. She turned on the lights and canvases of varying sizes surrounded them.

He searched for the beginning and walked toward the first painting. It was of an overbearing man forcing himself on a woman. The woman appeared to be crying. He saw three children in the background, crying, and three older men with their backs turned.

In the next painting, a baby was being ripped from the belly of the woman. A man was in the background, but it wasn't the same man as in the previous painting. Mallory moved to the next painting, which showed a boy hiding in the corner and the overbearing man hovering over him, blood dripping from his hands. In the next painting, two boys were falling in a pool and the overbearing man was holding a rod. Many of the paintings showed abuse, pain and blood.

When Mallory looked at the next painting, he choked. He remembered the event but for some reason couldn't feel the pain. The painting looked half-finished. The overbearing man was pouring some substance in the mouth of a badly beaten body. Mallory could taste the bleach in his mouth.

He looked over at Brielle as he moved to the next set of paintings. He saw the boy living in a dark cave with an old man. Mallory was confused. If the paintings were of his life, Uncle Mal would have been next. He should see a farm with animals. That's what he was supposed to remember, but were those memories or stories that were told to him? He moved to the next picture, where the old man stood over the boy as he studied what appeared to be languages.

The next sets of paintings were black scribble. "You lost your passion," he said.

The next two paintings showed a man fighting in his sleep and a black cloud hovering over him; then four men in suits, standing, with three looking up at one. Next, was a picture of a man standing at a podium talking to an excited crowd? The overbearing man was in the background, faded and old.

When Mallory moved to the next painting of a man dressed in bright celestial white, standing next to a man in black, he said, "This must be Matthew." The wings were detaching from the body of the man in white as he embraced the man in black. "He's my angel."

The next painting showed a destroyed room and one man standing over another man lying on a bed. A third man was holding the first man's hands as if he were begging. As he studied several more paintings of tragedy, he moved to a painting that showed one man holding another man's hand as he fought something in his sleep. He didn't remember this painting. He looked around and saw several blank canvases lying on the floor. He walked toward Brielle, who was sitting on an altar surrounded by three candelabras. He grabbed her hands and brought them to his face.

"Is this really of me? Is this my life?"

"Yes."

"It's painful."

"I know. I lived your sorrow. That's why I don't understand why you still do it."

"Do what?"

"You live as if you're human, by human rules."

"I don't know anything else." He held his head down.

"There is another way, but you reject it. That's why your family is rejecting you."

"It appears that my family rejected me when I was born."

"Once again, you and your father are living by human rules. You don't have to follow in his footsteps. You don't have to live his pain. You are better. Greater." She lifted his head. "You are even greater than Marc. Stronger, more fierce, more powerful, more charismatic." She brought his face to hers. "You can lead this family and the next generations. You have the power because it ends with you." She kissed him. "You have to be ready."

"I'm scared."

"I know. I can show you, but you have to go through it alone." She jumped off and led him to the altar. He reclined back, looking up to the sky. She lowered the lights, and the candles began brightening the room. She returned, clutching an old dusty book close to her bosom. He sat up and helped her up to the altar. She handed him the book and he glided his hand across the cover.

"I remember this book."

"This is my father's book."

"That's your father?" He pointed to the painting.

"Yes. He was drawn to you, and so was I. Mallory, we were your family for those years that you don't want to remember."

"I'm confused."

"There isn't much time."

"I'm tired of this bloody bullshit!" he shouted. "Everyone wants me to do shit, but no one explains anything to me. I'm not doing anything."

"I understand," She relinquished her excitement and took the book back.

He disappointed her and he hated the feeling. "I'm sorry." He took the book back and opened it. "It's in ancient Hebrew." He thought about Matthew.

"Do you remember the chant for crossover?"

"Vaguely but they were just words to me." He studied the words on the page.

"Oh, I forgot something. Read the book, I'll be right back." She jumped off the altar and disappeared in the dark.

While Mallory glanced over the book, memories of her father floated back in his mind. He was kind and gentle, but very distant. He recalled her father telling him stories of a great and mighty battle, stating, "*The bad guys must win some of the fights so the battle can go on. No one wants the battle to end, especially the good guys. After the battle, there is nothing else.*"

He removed all resistance and made himself ready to follow her command. "What do you want me to do?"

"Remove your clothes and lie back." She helped remove his shirt and guided him to his back. As he removed his pants, she straddled him then positioned him inside her. She took a black marker and drew a heptagram on his chest. He closed his eyes, not understanding what was happening. She grabbed a black candle and poured hot wax in the center of his chest. Mallory cringed.

She took a dagger and cut her finger, then lifted her finger and allowed the drops to fall to his chest. She placed her finger in his mouth, and he kissed it, licking the blood. She gently grabbed his hand and cut his finger, lifting it up and allowing the blood to drop on his chest. Then she kissed his finger, sucking his blood. Mallory noticed wind blowing around him but he felt nothing. The ominous cloud, the dark shadow, floated into the room. It circled around them and hovered over Mallory. His eyes grew wide when the shadow darted for him.

𝔐

Mallory woke up alone in the room. He sat up then quickly looked around. His attention was drawn to the corner where the dark shadow was waiting for him. He flew off the altar, picked his shirt up from the ground and ran toward the door. The dark shadow grew larger and then floated toward him. He wrestled with the doorknob, but it was locked. He started banging on the door, screaming and pleading. As the dark shadow floated through him, Mallory screamed louder. It disappeared through the door to the other side. He stepped back as the knob turned slowly. When the door opened, Brielle was on the other side.

"Mallory?"

"I need to get home." He flew passed her.

"What's wrong?"

"Where are my clothes?"

"Mallory stop! You need to ..."

"I don't need to do bloody shit!" he screamed. "I need to get home. Matthew's waiting for me."

"Matthew's not there. He's not coming home."

"He's coming home! He loves me ... he is coming. I'm not supposed to be here with you." He grabbed his pants and ran out toward the stairs. He stopped long enough to put on his pants, then looked up and saw the dark shadow standing between him and the door.

"I need you now, Matty." He closed his eyes, ran through the shadow, opening the door and running out toward his car. He stopped and covering his mouth. "My keys? Where are my keys?" He looked through the driver's window and noticed the keys in the ignition. "Oh thank you, Matty." He jumped in the car, turned the ignition and sped off as Brielle watched from the loft window.

As he drove off, Mallory closed his eyes and tried to recall what had happened. He looked through the rear view mirror because he felt the presence of the dark shadow following him even though nothing was behind him. Mallory wanted to escape somewhere safe but he couldn't remember where he lived. He didn't want to go to his father's house. He stopped at the light and banged his head on the steering wheel. He finally looked up and saw the hotel where he and Stacy stayed for their honeymoon. He drove in and threw the keys to the attendant. He rushed to the bar and slammed down on the barstool.

"Mr. Mallory, back so soon?" the bartender asked as he wiped the counter.

"Yes." He had no idea what the bartender was talking about.

"You're not tired of the little miss already, are you?" the bartender joked. Mallory shook his head as he patted his pockets. "How can I help you?

"Absolut, neat," he scratched his head. "Where's my cell phone?"

"Here you go ... do you want to start a tab?"

Mallory gulped the shot and handed it back. "Yes, if you give me the bottle." He handed him a credit card and the bartender returned with a full bottle.

"Be careful with that."

"I will." He clutched the bottle close, grabbing the glass, and walked to a table. He pulled out a chair and sat down slowly. He poured a tall glass of Vodka and gulped it down. He laid his head down on the table to calm his nerves, but he felt something bearing down on him. When he looked up, he saw the dark shadow and fell out of the chair.

He looked around the bar but no one saw the incident. He sat back in his chair, grabbed the bottle and started gulping it down. The faster he drank, the faster the dark shadow faded. He closed his eyes and forced himself to finish the bottle. When he opened his eyes, the shadow was gone. He stumbled back toward the bartender. "I need another one. I wasted this one."

"Now, didn't I say be careful." The bartender handed him another bottle.

"Whatever...you're charging me for the bloody thing," Mallory snatched the bottle and sat at another table. The dark shadow was sitting there waiting. "You're haunting me, are you? Why are you haunting me?"

The shadow didn't respond.

"What do you want from me? Got damn it, answer me!" He shouted and everyone started staring at him. "What the fuck do you want from me? Are you trying to drive me crazy?" He stood up, breathing heavily. "You think I'm going crazy, don't you? I'm not the only one who sees you. Everyone sees you." He stood up and started pointing at an empty chair. "He's haunting me. Right here...Now, you're exposed. I have exposed you."

The dark shadow didn't move.

Mallory resolved his obnoxious ranting and sat back in the chair, nursing his bottle. Hours passed and Mallory was still at the table ranting to himself. The bartender walked over to see if he needed anything.

"I need Marek. Call Marek?" Mallory pleaded.

"Who? I know your father; I can call your father," the bartender said.

"No!" He grabbed the bartender's collar. "Don't call him. I'll leave. I'll leave quietly." Mallory stumbled out toward the valet. "I need my car."

The attendant didn't move.

"What's wrong? You lost my car?"

The manager walked out and placed his hand on Mallory's shoulder.

Mallory jumped. "I just need my car."

"Sir, we can't give you the car."

"Why?"

"Would you like a cab?"

"Fuck a cab...I want my fucking car!" he shouted.

"Sir, we can't. I can offer to take you home or I can call your father."

"Give me my fucking car, now!" Mallory pushed the manager, but the manager politely stepped back and held his conviction. "Fuck you! I'll never come back to this bloody hotel again." He shouted out, stumbling back into the hotel and rushing into the bar. "Hey tender ... I can't find my cell phone. Can I use your phone?"

ℳ

The brothers and uncles were at Marc's estate waiting for Mallory to arrive. Just as Marc's anger brewed about Mallory's lack of concern, Marek sat at the table brewing with anger over Marc's attitude. Marc, pacing back and forth ranting obscenities about Mallory, eventually towered over Marek and began shouting down at him.

"You told him that he was supposed to come today, right? I told you that I wanted to talk to him last night. I don't even know if he is coming. We don't even know if he can do this. You wanted to handle him and look at this bullshit!" He continued his pacing. "This is bullshit. Dad, let's kill him. He's weak. Who says he can ever make it through this Proselytization? I barely did it. We all barely did it. It takes all of us to accept the shadow. One person can't do this. And we are all strong men. Mallory's a faggot." Marek jumped up and sucker punched Marc in the stomach.

"I warned you!"

"Did he fuck you or something? Is that the reason why you're sucking dick right now?" Marc pushed Marek against a wooden table.

"No! He's my brother. Just like you." He pushed him off. "I'm just wondering what gives you the right to determine who can be here and who can't. Dad can't even make that decision."

Malcolm stood up to confront Marek. "Watch it, Marek. I'm still your father."

"YEAH RIGHT! You're my father, but what about Mallory? You were there for me. But who was Mallory's father?"

"I was there for Mallory ..."

"BULLSHIT! Then you sent his ass away! He was so small; he had no fucking idea who he was. He came back at our request, but he still doesn't know who he is. We're supposed to act as if nothing happened, like he's just one of us. I have one got damn question ... why did we send him away?"

"It's not time for that discussion," Malcolm ordered.

"When is it time?" He shouted back at his father. "You all know why he was sent away, but no one will talk about it."

Uncle Mal and Malcolm bowed their heads.

"Okay...how 'bout this ... we're just going to accept the fact that he didn't get beat all those years." He stormed toward Malcolm, but Uncle Mal intercepted the attack.

"Stop, Marek! We all got it occasionally," Marc said as he grabbed his arm and twisted him around.

"Bullshit! I don't remember dad beating your ass because you took his Aston Martin out and crashed it when you were eleven. Mallory got it." He rushed over to Marlon, "Dad told Marlon not to get in the pool because it was too cold when he was eight. Mallory tried to help you get out. Dad beat his ass for that all night long. We all heard it! I used to drink all of Dad's liquor. Mallory got beat for that. He would crawl out of dad's room because he couldn't walk." He charged up to Marc again. "And now you want to take Dad's place? Is it that important for you to be the leader?"

"I'm the leader. Never question that." Marc matched his stance and threatened him. "You need to decide if you want to be a part of the family."

"Hell nawh! This is foul. You're foul." Marek pushed him away to walk away. "You're so scared of Mallory that you rather beat him down than to accept him."

"Why in the hell am I supposed to be scared of Mallory?"

"Cause he has already proven to be a better man than you wish you could ever be!"

A deathly silence filled the room.

"Marek, you said enough. Now sit down..." Malcolm said.

"Shut the fuck up, old man. Until you give me some answers, you don't tell me a got damn thing."

Malcolm went to charge up to him but Uncle Mal held him back.

"Fuck it! I'm out. I don't want this shit. You can take my charge."

"Marek!" Marc grabbed his arm again and squeezed it hard. "You know that we need you. You're the second strongest brother."

Marek snatched his arm back. "Who is the first ... you?" Marek's cell phone rang. "Who is this?" he shouted.

"Mawek! Mawek, it's me..." Mallory slurred on the other end of the line.

Marek didn't answer right away, finally jerking his arm from Marc's grip. He walked out of the dining room into the kitchen then closed the door. "What's up?"

"They won't give me my bloody car," Mallory slurred.

Marek could tell that he was drunk. "Who won't? Where are you?"

"I don't know." He started laughing hysterically. "I don't know. Somebody's following me."

"I need to know where you are." Marek shouted.

There was a loud thump then strange silence on the other end. The bartender picked up the phone and spoke briefly with Marek. Marek hung up the phone and headed to the front door.

Marc opened the dining room door to the kitchen and cornered Marek between the island and himself. "Where are you going?" Marc asked.

"Look, Mallory's not coming. I didn't tell him." He pushed him away. "I got better things to do."

"That wasn't Mallory, was it?"

"Now, why would Mallory call me? He thinks I'm like you."

"Okay. Look, I'm sorry. Mallory's presence has taken a toll on all of us. As soon as we alleviate him, we can get back to what we do best."

"Yeah, you running the show and me sitting on the sidelines as your personal bitch."

"Marek."

"I need to go." He stormed out of the house and jumped in his jeep. On the way, he called his wife. "Hey baby, can you be ready in twenty minutes?"

They finally reached the hotel bar, and Mallory was lying over a few bar stools. "Bro, what's up?"

"Hey!" Mallory tried to get up and fell off the stools. "Shit! I can't find my cell phone."

"Mallory let's go." Marek grabbed his arms and helped him to his feet.

"I can't. I'm waiting for Matthew. He's going to call me."

"Let's go, Mallory." He grabbed his arm but Mallory snatched it away.

"NO!" he shouted. "I need to wait for Matthew."

"Do you want me to call him?" Marek pulled out his cell phone.

Mallory nodded his head.

Marek called Matthew's cell phone and he answered.

"Matthew Peterson."

"This is Marek."

"Why are you calling me?"

"When was the last time you spoke with Mallory?" There was a dead silence. "This guy is fucked up and has been waiting for you to call him."

"I can't talk to him right now."

"You know what ... YOU'RE A BITCH! This guy is missing you and your punk ass can't call him."

"Marek ..."

"No, fucker, he's drunk and crying and shit and your bitch ass can't find two fucking minutes?"

"Is he okay?"

Mallory stumbled over to a lady at the bar. He leaned over on her, asking if she had any aspirin. The lady went into her purse and handed him two pills. Mallory grabbed her drink and started to chug the pills.

"Hell Nawh, muthafucka!" Marek knocked the pills out of his hands. "Don't give him shit! Can't you see that he's drunk?" He continued his conversation. "Do you see this shit? This muthafucka is trying to kill himself?" He pulled Mallory away from the bar and pushed him down on the chair. "Look Matthew, if you found some better dick, I think you need to tell him."

"It's not like that."

"I don't give a fuck what it's like. Talk to him!" He handed the phone to Mallory.

"Matty ... Matty? He's not there." Mallory handed the phone back to Marek and laid back down.

"Matthew!" There was a pause but he finally answered. "You know you're a fucking faggot." He shouted softly so Mallory couldn't hear him. "You stay away from him. You hear me? Stay the fuck away from him!"

"Marek, it's not like that. Put him in his shower. He'll be okay. Marek, I'm sorry."

"Me too." Marek hung up the phone and grabbed Mallory to walk out.

"Wait I need to close my tab."

Marek walked him over to the bar. The bartender handed him the bill and Mallory started to sign.

"What do I sign? Who am I? Mallory what ... Towneson? Haulm? Death. Oh, I know. I should do what the slaves used to do and sign an X." He laughed, throwing the pen and lying back on the stools.

"I'll sign it." Marek scribbled his name, collected Mallory, and walked out of the hotel. He managed to get Mallory to his jeep. He handed Jean the valet ticket to Mallory's car and kissed her on the cheek. "Look, I know I said I didn't want you involved in the family business, but I need you. Hide his car for a couple of days. If Marc calls, tell him that I'm –"

"Left with some skank ass ho," Jean quickly finished his statement.

"Damn, you said that too quick."

"It's not far from the truth."

"You know that I would never leave you, Jean. I might meet up with a slut, but I'll never leave you. And believe it or not, I do love you. I didn't start this war between us, you did! And I can't fix all our problems right now, but I'll start by forgiving you ..." He kissed her and trotted toward his jeep.

While Marek was driving to Mallory's house, he saw the dark shadow behind him. "Mallory," he shoved him, trying to wake him. "Mallory, wake up."

"We're home?"

"Not yet. What did you do last night?"

"I don't remember."

"Think."

"I can't!"

"Think muthafucka! What did you do? Where did you go?"

"Brielle's ... I went to Brielle's."

"Okay. And ..."

"I can't remember."

"Did she read anything or did you ... Mallory?" he shouted but Mallory passed out again. He stopped the car, turned to Mallory and tore his shirt open. He saw the symbol drawn on his chest. "Shit ... that smart ass ice bitch." He stood up in the driver seat and faced the shadow. "Not now! Not now ... Please, not now."

The dark shadow disappeared; Mallory started throwing up blood.

"Okay, we need to get you home." Marek jumped back in the seat and sped back on the road.

"Marek, you might think I'm crazy but there is something after me."

"I believe you. Let's get home." Marek sped into Mallory's driveway. He stopped short of hitting the garage door. He jumped out of the jeep and carried Mallory into the house through the back door. He rushed him to the bedroom and tried to put him in the bed, but Mallory refused.

"Matthew's not here. I don't need to be in here."

"Okay, let's take a shower."

"I'm not taking a shower with you, bitch. The last motherfucker I took a shower with broke my heart. You know, Matthew broke my heart before."

"Okay, then get in the shower by your got damn self. Can you do that?"

"Yes. I can do that. I miss him so much."

"Okay, come let's go." Marek helped him to his feet.

Mallory fell back on the bed. "Nobody loves me ... my dad hates me ... my brothers hate me ... even my mom didn't want me. Why didn't she just abort me if she didn't want me?"

Marek completely understood Mallory's meltdown but he didn't have any time to spare to console him; however, he knew Mallory was not going to cooperate if he didn't acknowledge his feelings. Marek fell to his knees and grabbed Mallory's hands. "She did want you. She wanted to take you with her. That's why she took all those pills. She wanted you to be with her. They just got to you first."

Mallory was still slurring his words, "She killed herself because of me?"

"No, because of Dad. She couldn't escape him. When she found out that she was having you, she wanted to save you from him but she couldn't. She loved you so much."

"She did?"

"Yeah. She used to let us rub her belly. She talked to you and read to you all the time. You used to kick her a lot. I felt it once. I thought it was strange then." Mallory sat up to listen as Marek continued, "Once I had my son, I realized that it was their way of communicating. You two communicated a lot. It's like you two had your own language."

"She did love me?"

"Yeah, a lot. Mallory I need you to take a shower. We don't have much time ... there are a lot of things I need to tell you. So can you hurry?"

"Okay." He stumbled to the shower, pushed the button and got in.

Marek rushed outside and put his car in the garage.

After he spent hours in the shower, Mallory strolled out of the shower and put on some of his lounging khakis and a cotton shirt. Marek met him in the living room. They sat on the couch at opposite ends and didn't speak to each other. Marek was fidgeting with a scared expression painted on his face that bothered Mallory.

Mallory turned to Marek and asked, "What's wrong?"

"What did you see?"

"A dark shadowy thing ... I couldn't shake it. What is it?"

"Your charge."

"My what?"

"Your charge, your power, your destiny."

"What does that mean?"

"Mallory, someone has unleashed it, and it's after you. There is no way to stop it."

"Well, I'm done up like a dog's breakfast," He mumbled to himself. "What if I don't want it?"

"It'll kill you."

"Bloody hell!" He fell back on the couch.

"Look, when I received my charge, everyone was there to help me. No one can take in the dark shadow by himself."

"What am I supposed to do, call Marc?"

"Marc won't help you. He would tell you to do things that will make the dark shadow kill you."

"Fuck ... what am I supposed to do?"

"I think I can guide you. I remember Marlon's conversion. Think ... shit ... think! Okay, lie back. You're supposed to be asleep."

"How can I sleep now?"

"Just relax. Oh and remember, don't fight it. Just let it flow through you."

"That's it?"

"I'm trying to remember this. I'm not good at this. Marc is better. He knows the steps and protocols and the chants."

"Chants? There is a chant?"

"Yeah, it's in..."Marek thought hard. "Not in English."

"Fuck! I should get my gun."

"You got bullets?"

"Fucking hell, Marek!"

"No, we can do this. The chant is in...name some of the languages in Bible."

"Arabic?"

"No."

"Latin?"

"No."

"Spanish ... French ... what?"

"Shit, I don't know."

"Languages in the Bible," Mallory tried to concentrate. "Hebrew?"

"Yeah that might be it."

"Hebrew or ancient Hebrew?"

"There's a difference?"

"Got damn. What does the chant say?"

"How the fuck should I know?"

"OH, GOT DAMN."

"Let me see...it will say the chant. You just repeat it."

"Are you sure? What if it asks me something and am I'm supposed to answer?"

"Oh shit, maybe that's what it is!"

"Oh Marek, I'm fucked."

"Yeah, you are. But you know the languages, right?"

"But I don't know the answers!"

"Just say yes to everything."

Mallory fell back laughing. "Oh Marek, I guess this is a good time to tell you that I love you."

"I love you, too, bro. We gonna get through this. You didn't come this far to end it here."

"I need a glass of wine."

"No no no, don't do that. That makes everything worse."

"Okay, just relax." Mallory laid down, trying to relax.

Marek sat back as well. "Where's your remote?"

"Right next to you? What are you going to watch?"

"ESPN."

"Damn...that'll put me to sleep."

"Do you do guy shit?" he fussed.

"Yes! Not couch potato shit. I do a lot of guy shit."

"Like what?"

"I play basketball, workout and I swim. I used to play rugby. I used to fuck women. Fucking Matthew is guy shit."

"That's gay shit." Marek spewed out and Mallory rolled his eyes. "You played rugby?"

"Yes, in college."

"That's like football, right?"

"Yes without the pads and helmet. I was good. Real good. That's how I met Matthew."

"He played?"

"He was varsity. Champion player. He was the best on the team."

"Shit, you pulled a champion player?"

"You know me, best of the best. Not all faggots are flames." he teased. "It didn't start out that way. We hated each other... couldn't stand being in the same room."

"Like you and Marc."

"I can stand being in the room with Marc. He can't stand me. This was worse. We almost got expelled from school because we were fighting in the library and knocked over, I think, three shelves of old dusty reference books. He knocked out two of my teeth and I cracked his jaw."

"Got damn. Y'all were fighting."

"Yeah," Mallory smiled. "It was always a brawl when we were together."

"What changed?"

"It's a long story."

"Well, it's four o'clock. Unless you're about to go to sleep in the next two minutes, you can talk about Matthew or watch ESPN with me."

"What choices?" he paused. "Marek, nobody knows this, but I had a little girl in college. She died...of SIDS, they say. The day after I buried her, Matty came by to visit. I don't know why he was visiting me. Anyway, he walked in and saw that I was drunk and crying. He dragged me in the shower and sat in there with me for hours. We finally got out, I took his wet clothes and handed him some sweats. I don't recall how it happened, but I think I kissed him ... and the next thing I know we were making out."

"That's some shit. I wish a muthafucka would try to kiss me. Fuck the damn dark shadow; I'll bust your ass."

"Eventually that's kinda what he did, aye?" Mallory scoffed at his choice of vulgar words.

"I would KICK your ass...throw you up against the wall or some shit," Marek corrected his sentence. He shook his head. "So how could you fuck your own brother?"

"We didn't know that we were brothers until graduation. We started the relationship in our sophomore year."

"You didn't know until graduation?"

"No. We attended school under our mothers' maiden names. I was Towneson and he was Peterson."

"That's fucked up."

"Once I found out, it bothered me but it didn't bother Matthew."

"He turned you?"

"I don't know. He would like to think that he did, but I don't think he was gay before. Maybe we turned each other. Two irresistible men...couldn't resist each other." Flowing thoughts of Mathew made Mallory relax. He began to yawn.

Marek turned the sound up a little. "Sleepy?"

"A little."

"Do you sleep hard?"

"Only after sex."

"Well you're shit out of luck." He laughed.

"I think I'll be okay." Mallory turned over and drifted off to sleep.

Marek snuggled on the chaise lounge watching sports highlights. He finally drifted off to sleep as well.

The wind started banging against the windows. A hard burst of wind broke open a window and the dark shadow crept in the room. The temperature of the room dropped dramatically and both men shivered.

It hovered over Mallory. He tossed and turned then began fighting. Marek finally woke up and noticed the dark shadow attacking Mallory. He saw Mallory fighting in his sleep.

Marek quickly grabbed his hand and yelled out, "Don't fight it. It will hurt more."

Mallory screamed out.

"Come on Mallory, listen to me. Don't fight. Just stay still."

The dark shadow darted through Mallory's body, lifting both of them up and throwing them off the couch.

"Shit! He's supposed to be restrained. Damn it!" He looked around to see if he could find anything to restrain him. Just then Harold walked in. "Who the fuck are you? Get out of here? Wait muthafucka. Grab his legs!"

"What's going on?" Harold kneeled down.

"I'll tell you later."

"Where's Matthew?" He finally grabbed one of Mallory's flying legs.

"Look, got damn it, shut the fuck up and grab his got damn legs." They finally restrained him but Mallory continued fighting and started spitting up blood. "Mallory stop fighting it. Mallory, listen to my voice. Listen! Stop fighting."

Mallory managed to stop tossing, but his body was still tense.

"Mallory, just relax. Relax, Mallory. I know it hurts, but just relax. Relax, Mallory. Relax, Mallory." Marek could see parts of Mallory's body loosening up. He noticed Mallory's breathing becoming shallow. "Mallory, listen to the chant and answer him." Marek closed his eyes and the words starting floating in his mind. He quickly shouted, "Mallory say this: *The words are spoken on this dark night, as evil spreads from which was light. I invoke the Gods, the powers that be; invoke the power to set me free. I call and accept my power, charge this night; I call my power, my birthright.*" He looked over and Mallory was reciting the words, in ancient Hebrew.

A stroke of lightning bolted in from the open window and struck him. His body jolted and he started fighting again.

"No, Mallory, stop fighting."

He managed to relax his body again. The dark shadow circled around him, and Mallory started panting again.

"Oh shit. It's about to get scary now." He looked over at Harold. "If you want to leave, leave now."

"I can't move." Harold whimpered out. "Should I leave?"

"It depends. Do you feel lucky?"

"Not really. I'll stay."

"Mallory, listen to me. We're going to have to let you go. Don't fight. Just relax. Listen to the shadow. Answer the questions. Don't fight. I'll be right here. Mallory, don't fight. Squeeze my hand if you understand me."

Mallory managed to squeeze his hand and Marek was relieved.

"I'll be right here, bro. I'll never leave you." He looked over at Harold. "Let him go." They slowly let him go. He started shaking and twitching. "He'll be okay."

Several spirits flew in, grabbed his body and lifted it in the air.

Marek shouted, "Mallory say this: *Forces of Power of dark and light, spirits of air, earth and sea, summoned the souls of darkest knights, invoke the death in me.*"

Bolts of lightning shot through Mallory and he laid still.

"That's it, bro."

A ring of light grew and exploded in the room, knocking out all power to the house.

Marek woke up to find Mallory's body shivering in the corner. He wasn't looking well. Marek picked him up and placed him on the couch. Harold woke up and managed to walk toward the chaise lounge. Marek placed his hand on Mallory's face. It was ice cold. "Do you know where he keeps his blankets?"

Harold nodded his head.

"Go get them."

Harold stood up looking at Marek. "Peter will be home soon. I don't think you want him here."

"I'll deal with that later. Right now I need those blankets." He turned his attention toward Mallory. "You're doing good, bro. Just stay with me. Stay with me, baby."

Mallory started choking and threw up across the room.

"I need them got damn blankets now!"

Harold finally returned with several blankets. Marek carefully wrapped Mallory up like a mummy. He laid next to him, holding him tightly.

Harold grabbed a bottle of whiskey and sat down next to them. "Is he going to be okay?"

"Yeah. He's a strong muthafucka. He's a Haulm." He said then thought, *all those years of abuse, only he could do it.* Marek kept a close watch while Mallory was going through his transformation.

Early that morning, Mallory finally woke up. He noticed Marek asleep, holding him tight. He managed to loosen the grip and slip out without waking him. He noticed Harold asleep as well. He walked toward the kitchen and noticed the lights were out and the clock flashed 3:30. He walked to the sink, turning it on the water and started drinking straight from the faucet. He stopped.

"What am I doing?" He went to the refrigerator and grabbed bottled water. He noticed the lights were off. "Why are my lights off?" When he huffed, the lights turned on. "Oh, it must have been a bad storm." Without thinking, he started cooking breakfast.

Marek ran in the kitchen to find Mallory talking calmly to himself and cooking. He looked up and smiled. "Hey Marek. Hungry? I'm starving."

"Are you okay?"

"I'm starving and cold but I feel fine. What time is it?"

"I don't know."

"I'll find out. Have you seen my cell phone?"

"Mallory, you destroyed the cell phone."

"How?"

"Over Marc's head."

"Damn, I must have been pissed."

"What was the last thing you remember?"

"Matthew leaving. I was angry. I need to call him. He said I would regret not walking him out. Oh man, I love him so much." Mallory flipped his bacon and checked his waffles.

"Mallory, you got married."

"No, that's in a couple of days."

"That was last week."

Mallory was shocked. "I went through with the wedding and married her? WOW! How was the wedding?"

"How do you do that?"

"What am I doing?"

Marek walked toward Mallory. "Stop. Stop cooking." Marek turned everything off and removed the pan from the heat. "Come here. Sit down. You really don't remember the last week?" He grabbed Mallory's arm and sat him down on the floor. "Mallory. Don't do this? I know you remember and I know that it's going to hurt. Come on...let's play this back." Marek grabbed his hands.

"I don't want to do this." He tried to retract his hands but Marek kept a tight grip on them.

"Mallory, I'll be here."

"For what, breakfast? I need my cell phone."

"Mallory, come on man. Don't do this?"

"What am I doing? What do you want from me?" Mallory started shaking and coughing black smoke.

"Mallory, listen to me. You're making it worse. I know that you want to forget everything bad that happened to you. Somehow, you found a way to block out shit, but you can't do that. Not this time, you have to remember. That's what makes you who you are." He squeezed Mallory's hand tight. "Come on, remember. Matthew left ... fill in the blanks."

"I didn't walk him out."

"Okay ... and ..."

Mallory shook his head.

"We were at the church ... Dad hitting you?"

He tried to retract his grip but Marek held his hands tightly.

"Come on Mallory! You couldn't fight him back...you were bleeding ..."

He slumped down, pulling his arms back and balling his fist.

"Come Mallory, remember...Marc hitting you. But you fought back that time."

Tears fell from his eyes.

Marek grabbed his hands again. "Come on Mallory, the dark shadow?"

His touch turned ice cold and Marek was unable to hold his hands. As tears fell from his eyes, ice drops fell to the ground.

Marek could see the events playing in his mind flash in his eyes. His eyes glared blue.

Marek felt the temperature drop drastically. "Mallory. Control it. Don't let it consume you. Control it."

He shook his head no.

"Yeah, you can. Come on baby, breathe." Glass began shattering and flying in the air.

Harold ran to the kitchen. "Put his ass in that shower!" Harold screamed out.

"What?" Marek said.

Harold ran past Marek and grabbed Mallory. "Put him in his shower or he is going to blow this place up!"

Marek grabbed his legs and they dragged him in the shower. "Okay? Then what else?" He dropped him on the floor.

"Pull this lever when I get out." Harold ran out of the shower, ducking glass and debris.

"What the fuck else?"

"Can you stand hot water?" Harold shut the shower door and turned the shower on.

Marek went over and pulled the lever. A second set of walls rushed down and the temperature heated up quickly. Marek stood in a corner and witnessed the torture that Mallory was enduring. The walls dented in the shower and the water temperature grew hotter. "He couldn't have gone through this at the library."

The walls were taking a serious beating as the shower spouts began shooting fire, but turned into ice before hitting Mallory's body. Marek couldn't stand the heat and started screaming for him.

"Mallory, you're hurting me."

Mallory stood up and walked toward Marek. He grabbed his arm and threw him in the corner.

"Mallory, I'm burning."

He walked toward him and stood over him. Marek stood up trying to shield himself from the fire.

"Mallory, help me?"

"KNEEL BEFORE YOUR GOD!"

Without hesitating, Marek kneeled and closed his eyes in fear, waiting for the fire spouts to hit him but they didn't. The rain showerhead sprinkled cool water and the second walls began lifting. Marek finally opened his eyes and looked around. He saw Mallory sitting in the corner crying and rocking himself back and forth. He eventually crawled over to comfort him. "Mallory?" He sat next to him and wrapped his arms around him.

Mallory rested his head on his chest. "I hate these feelings. I can't control them. I can't make them stop. I don't like it." Mallory mumbled.

"I'm sorry. Do you remember?"

He nodded.

"I can help you control them. Take my hand." Marek stood up and reached out for Mallory's hand. "It's okay. You're okay."

Mallory managed to stand up and they walked out of the shower together.

"Do you want anything?"

"Cold water."

Marek ran to the refrigerator and grabbed several bottles of water. He handed one to Mallory and he drank it slowly, staring at Marek.

"Hey can I ask you a question?"

Mallory nodded.

"You said Matthew was looking for the final?"

He nodded again.

SHIT! He can't be it, Marek screamed silently. He took a deep breath and then said, "You have a lot of talent and strength, but you don't know how to control it. You must think you have hurt a lot of people you loved and blocked it out."

Mallory started sobbing again.

Marek grabbed him and held him tight. "That's okay. I need to take you somewhere. I think you're ready."

"You didn't leave me."

"Hell nawh! I told you I wouldn't," he smiled. "I'm your big brother. You're one of us now."

CHAPTER FIFTEEN

Marek drove for hours as Mallory gazed out the window. Memories of fires and people falling dead at his feet flooded his mind. He closed his eyes and attempted to shut out the visions, but the images were crystal clear in his mind.

As he stood in front of the Haulm Industries building, it seemed different. It still was an old rustic building, but Mallory could see the history in camouflage. He followed Marek to the back of the building and down a set of rusty staircases. Marek waved his hand over a pad and a stone door opened. He walked in, but Mallory waited outside.

Marek walked back out looking for Mallory. "What are you waiting for?"

"Am I supposed to be here?" Mallory asked.

"Yeah, if you weren't, it would have killed you."

"I'm not walking in there."

"Damn Mallory!" Marek waved his hand back and closed the door. He pushed Mallory in front of the door. He grabbed his hand forcing him to wave it over the pad. The stone door opened again. "Are you happy now?"

"That doesn't mean a bloody thing to me!"

Marek pushed him inside. As Mallory stumbled in, he looked around the dark room that was filled with books and old paintings of battles. He saw bottles and containers of weird things floating in fluid substances.

"What's this place?"

"This is the Black Knighthood Library." Marek quickly climbed up another staircase then stopped, waiting for Mallory. "This is everything you need to know about who you are, who we are, and all the history and how the battle really started." He beckoned Mallory to follow him.

Mallory followed Marek up the stairs and through the corridors. He saw people in their offices working. He passed a conference room with monitors lining the wall. Above each column of monitors were names showing the designated department: Pollution, War, Famine and Death. He slowed down to view the monitors. Marek stopped once he realized that Mallory wasn't behind him. He quickly walked back toward him.

"That's our progression of the battle." Marek explained as he pointed to his section of War. "See, I'm at seventy-three percent. I'm trying to get to ninety percent. I need to start a war somehow. I'm losing the fucking war on drugs because of them damn parents taking an interest in their kids again. It pisses me off." He stormed off then yelled in the distance, "Come on Mallory."

Before he left, Mallory looked over at his monitors and saw his percentage. It's twenty-three percent. "Is that good or bad?"

Once he realized that Marek left him, he quickly ran off to catch up with him. He finally reached Marek when the scenery changed. He gazed up at the dark cherry panel walls and saw many pictures of past horsemen. He noticed that most of them were not black. "I take it that we didn't always have the charge?"

"Not always. Since Adam and Eve left the garden, God put us in pass to keep balance in the world. It passed down through many generations throughout Europe. We finally got the change to be horsemen through them damn slave drivers. To be a horseman is a high esteem. The spirits weren't happy with the horsemen who were involved with the slave trade. If them last fuckers knew that they could lose more than their rights to own slaves, they would have kept their dicks in their pants instead of raping our women. Them fuckers are pissed. They're trying to get it back, and our black asses are multiplying. And we follow the law – not getting in involved with human or angel battles."

"So, it follows the mother's line?"

"Yeah, kinda, it takes two."

"Well, shouldn't we stick with our women?"

"That's why we only marry and procreate with our chosen women."

"Stacy is Jewish."

"Stacy's step-father is Jewish... and a fucking asshole and a crooked politician. After he couldn't get re-elected because of that scandal, he sold his daughter to get on the board. I don't trust that son-of-a-bitch! We really need to get rid of him, but that will be your first task. You can't have too many chiefs in your tribe." Marek stopped short of the double doors and turned around. "Here's home, the headquarters, the real company," he announced.

"So we're not an energy company?"

"Yeah! You have to diversify, Mr. Financial Man. Many-great Grandpa Marlow knew that so he created this company centuries ago during slavery. It's a better disguise. It opens the doors for us to infiltrate."

"Infiltrate who?"

"Anyone we want. Everybody needs energy of some kind. We touch every aspect of a person's life. From water, air, fuel, food ... you name it."

They walked passed Marc's office. It was meticulous and clean. He had several air filtration systems and many plants. "What's up with this?" Mallory asked.

"Oh, he's worried he'll die of pollution or some disease. He likes his air clean. Hey, when you walk into his office, use that sanitizing shit or he'll freak out."

He passed by Marlon's office and saw diet books, health magazines on the shelf. "Is Marlon trying to lose weight?"

"Hell nawh! He's trying to bulk up. He has all of those diet plans so he knows what not to do. Don't mention anything about him looking smaller."

"Is he? He's always eating."

"I know. He thinks he's going to die of starvation. He cooks up here every Thursday. Man, his food is off the chain."

"What are you scared of?"

"I ain't scared of shit." He opened the door to his office. Mallory noticed a library of anger management tapes, books and posters.

"Not scared of anything, huh?"

"I'm just tryin' to keep my cool," Marek laughed.

"Okay. So if you're scared ..."

"I SAID I ain't scared."

"Concerned. Let's use the word 'concerned'. If you're concerned with controlling your anger, and Marc is obsessing over pollution, and Marlon of starving, what's death scared of?"

"Dying?"

"That's a train wreak I didn't see coming ..."

Marek laughed, "Yeah dying. It's one thing to know how you're going to die but not know when, but it's completely different if you don't know the time or the cause. I know I'm going to die from my anger, but you can die from a car accident, a freak accident, choking, a train wreak, or a son-fucking-his-brother-on-top-his-father's-desk-induced heart attack." They laughed. "You know that shit wasn't right."

"I apologized."

"Why? That's your job...to kill people and take their souls. I was trying to tell you to finish the job, but you just didn't know. Man, you had us confused. That's why everybody was mad at you. You did shit and didn't know it."

"So, where is my office?"

"Across the hall."

Mallory looked over and noticed Malcolm Haulm's name still on the door. "I guess you were thinking I wasn't coming."

"Nope. You missed nine Proselytizions."

"Nine?"

"Yeah. Dad thought that he wasn't going to be able to retire. He was pissed. When you finally came back, he packed quickly. He was ready to run the energy company. That's such a fucking cushy-ass job."

"You think running a multi-million dollar company is easy?"

"Yeah, I can run that bitch in my sleep."

Mallory sat on the couch in Marek's office. Marek turned on a Zen tape and started meditating. "Do me a lemon."

"What? Look, you gonna have to start speaking English, or at least Texan. Plus, I'm trying to meditate? I had a hard week dealing with you. Don't piss me off."

"Okay, so what do I do?"

Perturbed, Marek turned off the tape and grabbed Mallory's hand. He walked him over to his new office and waited for Mallory to open the door. Mallory slowly opened the door. He looked around before walking in. It was a dusty office with many books covering an antique wooden desk. He stepped in and saw an indention of missing paintings and pictures.

"Hey, I pulled some books from the library for you. You need to read the one in your seat first."

"What is it, Death for Dummies?" Mallory finally made it behind the desk and picked of the book.

"Funny, bitch. It's our family album. There is a picture of mom in it. I thought you might want to see her. She was beautiful. You look like her."

Mallory opened the book and saw her. She was beautiful. Although the picture was in black and white, he could see that her skin was a delicate honey brown. Her eyes were light in color and her hair was long and wavy. He sat down and ran his hands across her face.

"That's your book. She wrote something in there just for you."

"She did?"

"Don't think you're special, bitch. She did it for all of us."

Mallory flipped through the rest of the book and noticed the pages were blank. He looked up and noticed Marek's sad face.

"Yours is the worst. You have no baby pictures. Mine stopped when I was four."

"Can I see your book?"

"Sure. Later but now you have a lot of fucking reading to do, Angloland." He teased him, "I pulled only English books. I didn't know your ass was bilingual."

"Multilingual."

"Whatever, bitch? There are many books in all languages in the library. You might come across my books in there."

"You wrote a book?"

"I wrote six books."

"No shit? Tell me a title."

"How to Beat a Muthafucka Down," Marek said proudly with a smile.

"And you named it that?"

"Yeah! It's my bestseller. Them militia eat that shit up." They laughed. "They would piss fire if they knew a darkee wrote it." Marek started to walk out and Mallory called to him.

"Marek, you said that you went to a black school?"

"Yeah."

"A black knighthood school?"

"Hell Nawh, bitch. I went to Howard."

Mallory shook his head and Marek walked out of the office singing the Howard Alma Mater song. Mallory sat back and picked up a book. He brushed the dust off and the emblem of the book glowed. He slowly opened the book and started reading, but couldn't concentrate because of the noise outside. He looked up to check out the commotion, then he returned to reading, and the noise got louder. So, he looked up quickly and the door slammed shut. He was stunned. He shrugged it off and resumed reading.

Mallory sat back in his chair, squirming to get comfortable. He didn't notice but the chair started changing to conform to his body. He finally found a comfortable spot. He ran across the word angel and his mind wandered briefly to Matthew. He stopped reading for a moment when he noticed Matthew's favorite song playing in the background.

Marek returned and heard Luther singing. "What the fuck are you doing?"

"I thought I was reading, and Luther started playing."

"Yeah, okay. I forgot to tell you that you have power of thought. So be careful what you think about."

"Really?"

"Yeah, remember when you told me and Dad about that arbitrage shit?"

Mallory nodded.

"Dad and I both ran out of our offices butt-ass naked. That shit is psychotic."

Mallory's side began aching with laughter.

"That's too many got damn things happening at the same time."

"I'll be careful."

"I'm leaving. Are you going to be okay?"

"If I need you, I'll think about you," he smiled. Mallory finished the first book and grabbed another. He read the title, *"Shadows and Spells."* He opened the book and flipped the pages carefully. The chair changed from an executive office chair to a lazy boy recliner. He subconsciously grabbed for a glass of wine and it appeared on the small table next to his recliner. He looked around slowly and realized that he transformed the office to a replica of his office at Towneson Financial. He turned back and changed the window view to the landscape of Amsterdam, which made him content. He resumed reading and random thoughts of Matthew floated through his mind.

A female voice asked, "Would you like for me to command his soul for you my master?"

"No," he said. *I want his body*, he thought.

"My master, command his body?"

"No!" He rubbed his face and resumed reading. "Focus." He finished the third book and opened up the fourth. Marek walked in.

"Hey ... what the fuck?" He looked around.

"I'm a quick study," Mallory smiled.

"I wanted to tell you that Marc will be here in the morning. I don't know if you're ready to see him. If not ..."

"I'm not worried about Marc."

"Big shit now?"

"Anyway, you said that these books are in other languages?"

"Yeah, why? They say the same thing."

"Not all the time. When translating you can lose the original meaning?"

"No shit?" Mallory nodded. "Damn, Marc didn't know that."

"How could he? He didn't go to college."

"Okay wait ... don't bring that shit up. He'll hit the roof."

"Well no one told him to pop that ass before the wedding."

"Mallory, don't start no shit again. He said that baby was premature."

"Are you going to tell me that you can have a 9-pound premature baby?"

Marek grimaced.

"Whatever. Where are you going?"

"Yoga."

"Yoga?"

"Yeah, you two muthafuckas got me all wired and shit. I need to calm down. I ain't trying to die early. Fucking with you two got my pressure up."

"I appreciate your pressure being up for me."

Marek's faced relaxed a bit and he allowed a small smile to grace his face. "I'm glad you're here, bro. We needed you. We 'bout to fuck some shit up!" He screamed and it echoed out in the halls as he left the office.

Mallory turned the page and saw a spell to summon his mother. He jumped up to close the door and then read the directions carefully. He gathered and lighted two candles, creating a doorway to both worlds. He spoke the incantation in the book. The room grew cold and dark and the only light was from the two candles. He closed his eyes and waited. Moments later, a spirit appeared between the two candles.

"My love." a voice floated through the air.

"Mom?"

"My baby. You're so big and so strong. How are you?"

Mallory's heart dropped and his voice was frozen as her spirit transformed into a human body in front of him. Mallory stepped back, allowing her to step down off the table and she hugged him tightly. Tears fell from his eyes. "Why do you cry, my love?" She cupped his face and kissed his lips.

"I missed you so much. I need you, mom." He said in his softest baby voice.

"And I'm here. Tell me your worries. Why do you cry?" She embraced him softly.

"I don't know who I am and I don't know if I want this and I'm so scared." Mallory rambled childishly.

"I didn't want this for you, either. I wanted to take you with me, but they wouldn't let me." She grabbed his hands. "Lay with me my love."

Mallory followed her to the black leather couch. She laid down and held him close to her body. Mallory inhaled her vanilla and lavender scent. He looked into her hazel eyes flecked with blue. He touched her velvety soft face intimately with both hands. It was smooth and silky honey brown, just as he saw in the black and white picture. She was beautiful and she appeared not to have aged a bit.

"Oh my love. Your touch is irresistible. Just like your father. You're your father's child." She kissed him intensely.

He felt confused. *Is this supposed to be happening?* He thought. "Mom, why does he hate me?"

"He fears you."

"Why?"

"My love, our story is a tragic one." She unbuttoned his shirt. "I was promised to your uncle and we were very much in love. But your father spoiled his bride before the wedding."

Mallory thought, *Elysse, I wasn't supposed to sleep with her until we were married.*

"Yes, like your Elysse. You're your father's child. Don't follow closely in his footsteps." She kissed him again. He broke the kiss.

"What happened, mom?"

She looked in his eyes. "I was given to your father for marriage, but your uncle was very angry. He vowed that Malcolm would never find peace. Your uncle and I continued our love affair."

Mallory couldn't help but touch her face. She closed her eyes and inhaled his aroma. "You have an irresistible touch. You're your only father's son."

"His only son?"

"Yes my love. To earn highest favor with the Black Knighthood, you must have four boys to control the empire. Your father thought he was earning favor, so he forced me to conceive a fourth son."

"But you said I'm his only son."

"Yes, you are, my love. You're irresistible. Just like your father. You're your father's child." She kissed him again. He broke the kiss again and set back from her. "Mate with me for my revenge."

Mallory wanted to scream, "Shit no!" But this was his first time seeing his mother. "Mom, I don't think that would be right." He didn't want to look in her eyes or feel her disappointment. "Mom, does he know?"

"No, my love. He thinks that you're your uncle's son."

"Uncle Mallory? Is that why he named me Mallory?"

"How fitting. The one son that's not his,"

Mallory screamed silently again, *This shit is fucked up.* He looked at her. "Has she been reading my mind?"

"Yes, my love. I can read your thoughts and feel your feelings. You have your father's passion. Don't follow closely in his footsteps. I must leave you now. I love you." As she rose up, she kissed him. Mallory could hardly breathe. He felt himself slipping away.

As his breath escaped him he said, "I love you, mom."

CHAPTER SIXTEEN

After standing in the foyer staring blankly, Mallory finally strolled in the house, throwing the keys on the console table. He stopped at the mantle and gazed at the pictures displayed on the mantle. He noticed that the picture of Matthew was pushed aside to make room for the oversized crystal-wedding frame.

Without thinking, he quickly rearranged the pictures so Matthew's picture was front and center. He stepped back to look at it. The arrangement didn't satisfy him, so he removed the wedding picture from the mantle.

"That's better!" He continued his stroll to the bedroom. He stopped at the kitchen when saw Peter pacing back and forth, shouting to himself. He sat at the bar and watched Peter in the midst of an internal battle. Peter jumped when he felt Mallory's presence. He tried to smile but couldn't shake his peculiar look.

"Good evening, master Mallory. Stacy called for you."

"Is she all settled in school?"

"Yes, yes." He said nervously. "Would you like a glass of wine?"

Mallory was taken aback. Peter had never served him alcohol in the five years he worked for him. He shook his head no. Peter paused again, which increased Mallory's uneasiness.

He bowed his head then confessed, "Matthew's home."

"Really?" Mallory's face beamed with excitement. This was the best news he had gotten all week, but he couldn't understand why Peter was so despondent. "Where is he?" Peter wouldn't answer but Mallory forced him to. "Peter?"

"He's on the roof waiting for you. I'm sorry, master Mallory."

Mallory ran off to find Matthew and didn't hear Peter's apologetic sentiments. When Matthew left, it was on terrible terms and too much time had passed between them. Mallory wanted to apologize and gauge his anger.

Mallory flew up the stairs toward his office, stripping off his dress coat and flinging it on the floor. He ran to the window and flung it open. He stopped for a minute thinking about the past events. He worried that the new information he had would hinder their relationship. He turned back and started to close the window.

"But he's looking for The Final. I couldn't possibly be ..."

He opened the window and stepped out on the ledge then looked up toward the sky. There was an ominous dampness in the wind. The sky was dark and very cloudy, but Mallory didn't care. He hopped up the first step and climbed quickly. He finally reached the top to see Matthew sitting on a lounge chair with a sword lying by his feet.

"My angel!" Mallory shouted as he took great strides toward him, but Matthew never looked up. "Matty? Matty!" Matthew finally looked in his direction. "I missed you so much."

"Yeah, me too." Matthew's voice cracked.

Mallory sat on the lounge chair and grabbed Matthew, holding him tightly, but Matthew didn't hug him back. Mallory felt tears on his face. He pulled back and cradled his face, "What's wrong, baby?"

Matthew didn't respond.

"Look, whatever it is, we can fix it. I understand why you couldn't be at the wedding. I forgive you. Actually, there is no need for forgiveness. I love you so much."

"I love you, Mallory," Matthew said blankly.

"Mallory? You have never called me Mallory."

"Emerald, I'm sorry."

"Did something happen? You have to go back?" Mallory wiped the tears from Matthew's eyes.

"No more trips. I found all my answers," he answered coldly.

"Great! We can put all this behind us and finally work on our relationship."

"I guess," Matthew said, tears streaming down his face.

"Please tell me what's wrong?"

Matthew wouldn't look in his eyes.

"Matty, you're scaring me. Tell me. If I did it, I'm sorry." Mallory tried to hold back his tears as more tears fell from Matthew's eyes. "I'm sorry." Matthew handed Mallory an overstuffed accordion folder. "What's this... your research?" Matthew nodded. Mallory carefully unraveled the red yarn from the secured tab and opened the file, pulling out scrolls, articles and handwriting notes. "This is what I translated, aye?"

Matthew nodded his head.

Mallory scanned through scrolls and handwriting notes, then pulled out Matthew's handwritten notes and began reading them. "I don't understand."

"Pale face and piercing eyes," Matthew started reciting the painfully rehearsed information from the file. "You have gorgeous vanilla skin and the most beautiful and irresistible emerald eyes." He paused, "that turn ice blue when you're angry."

Mallory flashed a frown but Matthew wouldn't make eye contact as he continued.

"Not of woman born...is a woman who had a caesarean." Matthew thumbed through the file and pulled out Mallory's medical records. "They had to cut your mother open because she died in childbirth."

He looked back at the files while Matthew continued to read it aloud. "Unproductive man...is a man who can't produce offspring."

"By defect?"

"Or by choice," he paused. "Mallory, why didn't you tell me that you had a vasectomy in college?"

"I didn't think it was any of your business. It's not like we can have kids together. Don't call me Mallory."

"We talked about being fathers and having kids and raising them together."

"I figured that it would be you who would have them."

"Damn Mallory."

"STOP CALLING ME MALLORY!" he shouted. "I'm Emerald, your Emerald. I'm not this. I didn't ask for this. I just want to be with you. Matty?" He grabbed his arms prying them open but Matthew clenched them tighter to his body. "Matty, just hold me." Mallory grabbed his face, forcing Matthew to look at him. "Matty, I'm your Emerald."

Matthew finally looked into his eyes and gave a half-grin. "Yes, you are my Emerald."

"I don't want to be this. I just want to be with you."

"You are this. We are who we are and we can't change that."

"Yes we can. We can run away...go somewhere ... anywhere. Look, I'll give up the company; the board position, anything just to be with you."

"I have given up so much. I probably lost my Father's respect and love."

"Well it's my turn now. Our father never loved me anyway."

"No Mal ... Emerald. It's my fault. I fucked this all up."

"Your fault? You regret falling in love with me? You regret us?"

"No baby, I don't regret that. Oh God." He sighed deeply, "My Father sent me on one assignment and I fucked it up." Matthew sat back and threw his hands on his head.

"Malcolm will understand. You can lie to him and he won't know."

Matthew laughed and wiped his nose. "Emerald, you're so wild. Oh God, I don't know how to fix this."

"Stop calling Him. He can't help. We can talk to Malcolm together. We'll make up something. You and I are always great together, remember?"

Matthew shook his head then announced, "Malcolm is not my father."

Mallory frowned in confusion. "He's not?"

Matthew shook his head.

"So, we're not brothers? See, that's one good sign, aye?"

"My Father sent me on an assignment to kill the final fourth," Matthew kept repeating.

"Who is your father that would make you do some shit like that?"

"God." Matthew said quietly against the thunderous boom in the background.

Mallory's became paralyzed with shock. He couldn't comprehend this tidbit of omnipotent news. Several deadly moments passed, Matthew waited for Mallory to explode. He felt

Mallory's cold eyes burning through his skin, so he looked down. Mallory rose from the lounge chair, glared over him and completely changed his tone. "So you're telling me I have been fucking God's son?"

Matthew hesitated then nodded yes.

"I'm glad that you didn't come to the wedding. I could have ended up being His son-in-law. He would have shit a brick then." Mallory began pacing back and forth, screaming obscenities. "This is crazy! This is sheer insanity. And you thought what I did in Amsterdam was psychotic?!? This is...I don't know what this is."

"Mallory, this is all my fault. You have every right to be angry ... just don't be angry with Him."

"Angry with you? I can't be angry with you." Mallory kneeled down and grabbed his face. "I love you. It's Him. It's His fucking little twisted game He plays."

"He doesn't play games, Mallory."

"HE DOESN'T PLAY GAMES?" Mallory's tone changed vehemently again, "OH...OKAY! One day He gets fucking bored and decides to create man. Puts them on a paradise and fucking teases them to death. He gets mad at them, throws temper tantrums and kills His own creations with fire and water and every fucking thing He can think of? That's not playing games?"

"No. Humanity has —"

"Fuck humanity! They don't have a chance. This is His creation. His pile of shit. His problem. His fault. What chicken-shitter would send his son to kill me?"

Matthew shook his head.

Mallory's mouth grew wide once he heard his own question. "Oh wait ... you're not the first son He sent to fix His fuckups."

"MALLORY STOP! THAT'S BLASPHEMY!"

"BLASPHEMY?" Mallory screamed at the top of his voice. "What is He going to do? Strike me down? Kill me? Now if He could that, if He were capable of that, HE WOULD HAVE NOT SENT YOU!" He shouted against the thunder echoing across the sky.

Matthew shot up, "Give me a reason!" Matthew's sword hovered inches from Mallory's neck. Their eyes locked. In the midst of the hot humidity, ice frost that escaped Mallory's body sent chills through Matthew as a streak of blue lightning flashed across the sky and in Mallory's eyes. This was not the time for a battle and Matthew knew it, so he lowered his sword and said, "He gave me an assignment, and I fucked up. It's not His fault."

Mallory finally turned his attention to the sword in Matthew's hands. Although the sword was lowered a bit, Matthew was still ready for an attack. Mallory looked deeply into Matthew's eyes and said calmly, "So will it make you feel better to complete your assignment?"

Matthew was confused. He didn't understand where the conversation was going.

"You're here to kill me, aye? I'm right here." Mallory fell to his knees. "Kill me baby. I'll make it easy for you because I love you. I have supported you through your search, and I'll support you to the end because I love you." Mallory stretched his arms out and closed his eyes, "Kill me!" Mallory held his breath as he felt the cold steel tap his neck several times, but he released it when he heard the steel clash on the rooftop.

Matthew kneeled down to grab Mallory and screamed, "I can't do it!" Mallory opened his eyes and saw that Matthew had come completely unglued. He had never witnessed Matthew so broken and tormented. He wrapped his arms around and held him close.

"I love you so much. I wasn't supposed to touch you or look into your eyes. But I did and I fell in love with you." He bowed his head, "Emerald, when I saw you, I was in awe. I never felt love, not human love, before...you were the closest to human that I had even been associated with. I just wanted to be in your presence. When I touched you, I just craved you. I crave your human touch and your human spirit. I just wanted to feel human like you. You make it seem so easy, open, and free. I just wanted to be next to you all time."

Mallory wiped the tears from Matthew's eyes, "I always said that you were my angel."

Matthew looked up and smiled a little.

"I craved you, too. I didn't understand why until now. I guess it was your eternal spirit, your eternal life force. I was cold and empty and I just wanted to feel warm and complete. You did that for me." He held Matthew's chin up and looked in his eyes. "I love you, baby. I would never want to see you in pain. What do you want me to do? I can take your pain away if you just tell me what you want me to. Anything!"

The lightning thrashed across the sky as they embraced each other, with the defeating notion that this would be the last time they would be together. Although the rain started falling in sheets, Matthew eventually stopped crying and his tears were replaced with raindrops as he kissed Mallory softly.

He whispered in Mallory's ear. "Will you make love to me?"

Mallory looked at his eyes and flashed a fake smile. He placed Matthew's head back on his shoulders and angrily glared up to the heavens. Matthew gathered his composure and stood up. Matthew climbed down the stairs and Mallory followed him closely. When they climbed back through the window, Mallory stopped and stood at the window, staring up to the heavens. He tried to envision God's face through the rain.

"Is something wrong, Emerald?"

"Do you think you'll be here in the morning?"

"I don't think so."

"Is He waiting for you?"

"Yeah, but He can wait." Matthew flashed a morbid grin as he grabbed Mallory's hand and made their way to the bedroom. Mallory slowly opened the double doors and they walked in together. Mallory flopped on the bed and blankly stared out of the window. Matthew quickly headed to the window and closed the drapes; he didn't want Mallory to change his mind. He stood in front of Mallory, waiting for his signal to touch him.

Mallory finally looked up and smiled, grabbing Matthew's hand and kissing his fingertips. Matthew sat in his lap and began undressing him slowly. Mallory laid back, allowing Matthew's weight to consume his resistance. He closed his eyes, feeling Matthew's lips caress every inch of his body. The words of the scroll began to appear in his mind. Piercing eyes ... tortured soul ... skin of ice ... unproductive ... not of woman ...

Matthew made it back up to Mallory's lips and they kissed passionately. Mallory flipped him over and looked in his eyes. He saw the last line of the scroll in his eyes. *His greatest love is his enemy.*

Matthew mouthed, "I love you" but what Mallory heard was *"Beware, he will come as a thief in the night and slash thy heart."* Matthew grabbed Mallory's face, kissing him hard and wet.

"You're my greatest love," Matthew whispered in his ear with his eyes closed. Unbeknownst to him, his breath was frost and his hot touch cooled quickly on Mallory's skin.

Is it my heart or his heart that will be slashed? Mallory thought as he lowered down to kiss him, and ice tears fell from his blue eyes.

Author TL James
Literary classics with a contemporary swagger.

The Complete Saga

Other Titles

To learn more about the author or to read other excerpts from these books, visit www.authortljames.com.

PLEASE LEAVE A REVIEW!